GW00693615

THE GUILTY PARTY

Detective Chief Inspector Dick Tansey is bored. After weeks in hospital recovering from injuries sustained in his last case, he had been relegated to a desk job at headquarters, when all he really wants is to get back into the action. So he's only too happy to investigate a series of attacks on the aristocratic Rocque family. Initially minor in nature, these are escalating in violence and soon someone might be seriously hurt, even killed.

Why should the inoffensive Rocques be attacked? Is there a connection with an earlier unsolved, tragic hit and run case in which a schoolboy died? Tansey must get to the truth before tragedy strikes again.

THE GUILTY PARTY

John Penn

HarperCollins*Publishers*

36565163

Collins Crime
An imprint of HarperCollins*Publishers*
77–85 Fulham Palace Road, London W6 8JB

First published in Great Britain
in 1994 by Collins Crime

1 3 5 7 9 10 8 6 4 2

© John Penn 1994

The Author asserts the moral right to be
identified as the author of this work

A catalogue record for this book is
available from the British Library

ISBN 0 00 232535 7

Set in Meridien and Bodoni

Photoset by Rowland Phototypesetting Ltd
Bury St Edmunds, Suffolk
Printed and bound in Great Britain by
HarperCollinsManufacturing Glasgow

PART I

1

Frankie Carton pedalled hard. He knew that if he could gain enough momentum going down the hill he would be able to ride all the way to the top of the long gruelling slope ahead. He had done this every day, five days a week, for the last two years, often in rain and sometimes in snow, when he had been forced to push his bike. It was five miles from his home to Coriston College, and by now the journeys there and back had added up to a considerable distance. Frankie wasn't sure that the trips were worthwhile.

When he was twelve he had won, to his father's delight, a scholarship to Coriston. At the time he had been pleased too, proud of his achievement, though he had been perfectly happy at his comprehensive school in Colombury, a Cotswold market town not far from Oxford. But his pleasure had been short-lived. Coriston had proved to be a mixed blessing.

He was a natural scholar and he enjoyed the work, the stimulus provided by small classes and individual teaching. The compulsory games didn't bother him — he was a fair athlete — and the extra-curricular activities were geared to boarders and scarcely affected him. What he disliked, apart from the ten-mile ride in bad weather, was the feeling of exclusion. This was partly due to the fact that he was a day-boy in a predominantly boarding environment, but mainly because of the patronizing attitudes of his contemporaries.

When he had first arrived at Coriston he had been surprised by the questions he had been asked. What prep school did he come from? What did his father do? What cars did they run? Where did they go for their holidays abroad? One boy had even wanted to know if his parents hunted. He had answered all these questions truthfully; it never occurred to him to do otherwise.

His father, he said, was a writer; he wrote articles on politics and economics for various journals and magazines. His mother was dead. They didn't run a car. He had never been abroad; he and his father always went to Scotland to stay with his aunt for their holidays. As for hunting, his father considered it a cruel sport.

He hadn't enjoyed the amusement and feigned amazement that his answers had aroused, but he accepted them in good part. It was only when his father's arrival on a motorbike for the school play at Christmas had been greeted by a clapping, cheering claque that his resentment had aroused violent feelings. From then on he spent as little time as he could at Coriston, refusing to take part in extra activities and concentrating on his work.

But today was Friday, and it was the beginning of the half-term exeat. Frankie pedalled faster as he thought of the week ahead of him, helping his father with the household chores and the garden, going for walks – no cycling – reading, listening to music, being lazy. He didn't care a damn that a school party was going to Austria, or that Tristan Compton-Smith was joining his father, the British High Commissioner in Nigeria. He was quite happy with his own lot.

By now he had reached the end of the uphill grind. The rest of the way home was on the flat, and he should have been able to relax. The road was narrow and winding, but there was very little traffic; it was too late in the season for tourists and too early for any pre-Christmas activity. Unfortunately it was late. Mr Hauler had kept him talking.

He wondered about Jocelyn Hauler. One of the prefects, who had had an elder brother up at Oxford, had said that Hauler had been disappointed to get only a second-class degree and, knowing he had no hope of a fellowship, had taken the year's teacher training course and then gone straight to Coriston. He had arrived at the same time as Frankie, from which Frankie had worked out that he was probably twenty-two or twenty-three, by far the youngest of the staff.

But he was a good and conscientious teacher. Frankie liked him and had every reason to be grateful to him. Although Hauler officially taught English, on learning that Frankie's Latin was weak since the subject hadn't been taught at his previous school, he had volunteered to give Frankie some Latin coaching. It was a generous offer. Frankie appreciated it, but he did wish that Hauler wouldn't keep him chatting after the lesson. Today, with the long half-term ahead, it had been particularly frustrating.

Frankie continued on his way. The road here was at its narrowest, but still wide enough to allow two vehicles to pass each other with care, and it didn't bother Frankie when he heard a car approaching fast. He kept well over to his side and cycled on.

Frankie couldn't have described exactly what happened next. He was aware of a large red shape roaring around the corner on the right of the road. Then his bicycle seemed to disintegrate beneath him. His satchel flew over his head. He was lifted up into the air, to fall with a dreadful dull thump on to the bonnet of the car and roll off into the ditch.

The car made no attempt to stop. It rushed on as if oblivious of the trail of damage it had left behind it.

And Frankie lay where he had fallen, one leg twisted unnaturally under his body. He was conscious – just. He knew that he had been hit by a car. He knew that he was badly hurt. He knew that his cycle was in pieces and the contents of his satchel, which had broken open, were scattered along the hedgerow. All this he accepted. What worried him was the thought of his father waiting for his return and getting more and more perturbed when he didn't appear. He willed the people in the car to hurry back to help him.

It was minutes before he realized that the car had driven on, that it was not coming back, that no immediate help was in prospect.

Gavin Brail was the first person at the scene of the accident. Brail was thirty-five, a big chap, overweight, with a lot of

11

black hair and an incipient bald spot at the back of his head. He lived in Colombury with his wife and their two children, and worked at the Windrush Garage. Mr Field, the garage's owner, was not happy about Brail, though he couldn't have said why; Brail was an excellent mechanic, who more than earned his salary.

On this particular afternoon, work being slack, he had been dispatched on his motorbike to deliver a spare part to a small garage in one of the outlying villages. The weather was good. He had no need to hurry and he had been riding at a pleasant steady pace when he was overtaken by a red Toyota.

The Toyota caused him to swerve and, swearing at the driver, he shook his fist at the departing car. He was only seconds behind it and, though he didn't hear the sound of the crash because of the helmet covering his ears, he had no doubt who was responsible when he rounded the corner and came on the scene of the accident. No other vehicle had passed him, and there had been no side lane from which another car could have emerged.

He braked to a halt but remained on his bike, letting the engine tick over as he surveyed the scene, the tangled heap that had once been a bicycle, the scattered school books, and the poor, pathetic body half in and half out of the ditch. It didn't occur to him that the boy might still be alive; he had seen fatal accidents before.

'The shit,' he muttered. 'He might have stopped. I wish I'd taken his number. I'd damned well have reported him. Probably some rich prick, half drunk.'

Then an unpleasant thought occurred to him. If someone were to drive up behind him there would be no evidence to prove that he himself hadn't killed the boy. He couldn't imagine that the guy responsible would come forward to prove him innocent.

He rode on slowly for fifty yards so as to avoid the debris strewn in the road, then accelerated away on his errand.

Frankie had heard the motorbike and it had raised his hopes. He had tried to cry out, to show that he was alive and needed help, but no sound came. Only a thin stream of blood ran from his mouth and trickled down his chin on to his collar. As the motorbike departed and the sound faded into the distance, tears filled Frankie's eyes.

He was going to die here, alone. And what would Edmund do without him? Frankie knew that he meant everything to his father. He couldn't abandon him. After all, it wasn't as if he were in any pain; it was merely that he could no longer feel his body.

With a great effort Frankie Carton managed to raise himself and inch by inch crawl out of the ditch, to lie in the road.

As chance would have it, Frankie was found by Dr Band. Dick Band was the senior police surgeon for the district. He was of retirement age, but had been persuaded to stay on at the post for another three years. He hadn't taken much persuading. On the whole he enjoyed his work.

Band never drove fast; he had seen too many road accident victims in his time, and believed that no crisis merited the risk of adding a second emergency to a first. So, although the sight, as he rounded a corner, of a young boy lying in the road startled him, he was easily able to halt before reaching the body.

In spite of his age and a slight lameness due to rheumatism, Band was out of his car in seconds. He had switched on his warning lights and, giving Frankie a hurried glance, he seized the orange cones he always carried in the back of his car and ran to put two around the corner behind him and two a hundred yards in front of the accident, thus ensuring that no one would come upon it unawares and cause more mayhem.

Then he turned his attention to the victim. But his suspicion was soon confirmed. The boy was dead. He had died perhaps twenty to thirty minutes earlier, almost certainly of internal injuries which had caused a hæmorrhage. There was nothing that Band could do for him.

Once more he returned to his car and his radiophone. He spoke to Sergeant Donaldson at the Colombury police station, explained the situation and requested police assistance and an ambulance. He said that he had come on the accident by chance, but to him it had all the appearance of a hit-and-run case.

'Yes, of course I'll wait till you get here,' he snapped and thought with regret of old Sergeant Court, whom Donaldson had replaced; Court had become slow and lazy, but he would never have made a stupid request like that. 'It shouldn't take you long.'

While he waited, Band decided to discover, if possible, the identity of the young boy lying in the road. It was obvious from what he was wearing – his tie and the school crest on his blazer – that he was a student at Coriston, and presumably not a boarder, or he wouldn't have been cycling away from the college. But surely more could be learnt about him without searching the body. The sooner it was known who he was, the sooner his unfortunate parents could be informed of the tragedy. Band imagined them looking anxiously at the clock, asking themselves where their son could be, waiting and waiting for the boy who would never arrive.

Among the contents of the broken satchel that had been scattered about the scene were what looked like a couple of exercise books. Band picked one up. On the inside of the cover a label had been pasted. It read: *Francis Carton. Form IV. English. Set A. Mr Hauler.* Band leafed through it. The contents didn't interest him, though he noted that Francis Carton had consistently gained high grades and complimentary comments. What interested him were the initials at the end of the longer comments – *J.P.H.*

He wished he could remember what Patrick, his nephew, had called the Hauler with whom he had shared digs at Oxford two or three years ago. John? James? Band could think of no name that seemed to fit, and he told himself it would be absurd to assume the two Haulers were one and the same, even if they did happen to share a first name, as well as a surname.

Nevertheless, though he couldn't believe the schoolmaster had had anything to do with the boy's death, the surname intrigued him. Patrick had told him the story in confidence, how he had come back to his digs unexpectedly to find

Hauler in bed with a young boy from the town, and how after a row he had packed and left the digs.

'I don't care a damn what he did,' Patrick had said. 'That was his business. But I didn't intend to get involved, and possibly be sent down because of it.'

It could be an odd chance, Dick Band thought, if the dead boy had been a pupil of the man Patrick had known at Oxford. He hoped this wasn't so. He didn't like the idea of a schoolmaster who had a predilection for small boys. But it was not really his business, and he dismissed the idea as he heard in the distance the sirens of the approaching police convoy.

2

Christopher Portman waited until the front door had closed behind Alice Marsh, the Rocques' elderly housekeeper, before he walked around the Toyota and inspected it carefully. The car was three years old. It was in good condition, but in its time had sustained a few bumps and scratches. Only one looked vaguely new – that could be dealt with in his own garage – and the bonnet which he had feared might be badly dented from the weight of the boy's body was unmarked; the boy, he thought sadly, must have been very light.

With a strange feeling of reluctance, Portman got into the car and drove down the rutted drive of Wychwood Manor to the road. When he reached the rusting gates, which always stood open, he hesitated. By going a mile out of his way he could reach his own house without passing the scene of the accident. But that would mean waiting for information, and he would rather know.

Christopher Portman, like many self-made men, was a mixture of the practical and the romantic. At the moment his practical perspective was uppermost, or so he believed. He accepted that it had been a dreadful mistake not to have stopped, not to have gone back at once to see what could be done for the boy. That, however, was past history. What was the present situation? It would be wishful thinking to expect that the boy had collected his possessions, abandoned his ruined bicycle and gone limping home. It was more realistic to hope that he had been not too badly hurt, and was on his way to the promise of care and comfort in the hospital. The worst that could have happened was that he had been killed, which would mean that the driver of the hit-and-run vehicle – if caught – was liable to a considerable term of imprisonment.

'Best to know,' he muttered to himself, turning the car in the direction from which he had come.

It didn't take him long, even at a sedate pace, to reach the scene, and he had already seen the police cars ahead and slowed to a crawl before a local constable whom he knew slightly waved him down. He put his head out of the window.

'What is it? An accident?'

'Yes, Mr Portman, sir. A bad one. A boy from Coriston knocked off his bike and left to die. The bugger didn't bother to do anything about him. I expect he just drove on. Typical hit-and-run.' The officer obviously felt strongly.

'Would it have made any difference if he had stopped?' Portman asked.

The officer looked at him curiously and Portman realized that it had been an unusual question. How could the officer give an answer? Neither of them paid any immediate attention to the man on the motorbike who had just drawn up beside the Toyota and removed his crash helmet, and was listening to the conversation.

'Dr Band said not. It was Dr Band what chanced to find the poor lad. But he didn't die instantaneous. At least he could have had someone's arms around him.'

Portman nodded. He couldn't speak. He felt physically sick. The picture the officer had drawn had been too vivid. Anyway, he didn't need to ask the boy's name and address. The accident would be reported, at least in the local paper, and, although it was too late to help him, it might be possible to do something for his family, especially if there were other children.

'I'm afraid you can't go through this way, sir.' The constable turned to the man on the motorbike. 'Or you either, sir. We've closed the road for the moment, while we take some measurements and photographs. Luckily there's very little traffic along here.'

'You might be able to trace the car then?' Portman said,

keeping his voice steady. He hoped the officer couldn't see that he was sweating. 'And find the culprit?'

'We'll do our best, sir, but unfortunately the odds on catching him aren't good. Now, if you'll back up to the first left hand turning, you can rejoin this road in half a mile. I'll lead you, in case something drives up on your rear.'

'Thanks, Officer.'

There was no problem backing, past the entrance to Wychwood Manor, and soon Portman was driving along the alternative road, the road he had been tempted to take in the first place. He was glad he hadn't. Lost in unhappy thoughts, he paid no attention to the motorbike which was following a hundred yards behind him.

Portman drew up in front of the gates of Charlbury Hall, a property he had bought some nine years ago. It was a fine old house in ten acres of land, and had not been cheap at the time. Since then he had spent serious money on it, modernizing the interior and landscaping the grounds. He didn't care that the house was much too big for an unmarried man without a family. It was his pride and joy, and he used it to impress foreign associates, whose compliments on the place always pleased him. Besides, having installed a computer terminal he was able to do a lot of work from the Hall – his home.

For this reason, and because he had valuable furniture, pictures and antiques, he had done his utmost to make the house and grounds burglar-proof. He had installed an expensive anti-intrusion system inside and out. Alarm wires ran along the walls which encircled the estate. A guard patrolled the grounds at night. The wrought iron gates to the drive were electronically controlled.

It was the last point that was now causing Portman momentary annoyance. In any of his own cars he could have pressed a button and the gates would have opened, but this was Bertram Rocque's car. Not for the first time that day he cursed himself for having agreed to what had originally been a stupid arrangement, and which had turned out to be disastrous. He got out of the Toyota and pressed the bell beside the gate pillar.

'Mr Portman's residence,' a distant voice answered.

'It's me, Stanhope. Open the gates, please.'

'Yes, sir!'

Turning to get into the Toyota again, Portman saw that the man on the motorbike had stopped twenty-five yards behind him. Irritably he waved him on, and thought that if the chap didn't know the way and got lost in the lanes it was none of his concern. It didn't even occur to him that there might be another reason for the man to be making no effort to pass. The gates opened and Portman accelerated up the drive and around the house to the garages. He parked the Toyota. He would deal with the minor scratch later. At the moment, what he needed was a stiff whisky, and a long cool think about the possible consequences of the mess he seemed to have got himself into.

As the gates of Charlbury Hall closed automatically behind Christopher Portman, the man on the motorbike – who was Gavin Brail – rode slowly past. His mission completed, he had been returning home to Colombury when, to his surprise, he saw the red Toyota ahead of him. Convinced that this was the very car that had knocked the schoolboy off his bike, he guessed that the driver, in choosing to take again the road on which the incident had occurred, had been influenced by the same feeling as himself – curiosity as to what had happened to the boy.

It was curiosity of a somewhat different kind that made Brail continue to follow Portman, although originally he had no choice but to take the same diversion, and he was intrigued when the red Toyota stopped in front of the gates of Charlbury Hall. He knew the house and he knew the reputation of the owner; it was common knowledge in the district that Portman, though of humble origin, was a wealthy man who didn't give himself any airs. It was not unlikely, Brail concluded, that Portman should choose to drive a nondescript, slightly battered car, when he could have afforded what he, Gavin Brail, could only dream about. It was a pity he did not know Portman by sight.

Of course, there was no guarantee that the driver of the

red Toyota had in fact been Christopher Portman. It was unfortunate that he had arrived on the scene too late to hear the beginning of the conversation between the driver and the policeman. The policeman had, however, seemed fairly deferential. Nevertheless, the driver could be making a delivery. He could have business at the Hall. He could even be one of the staff. There were many possibilities. But remembering the manner in which the man had unhesitatingly rung the bell and, when the gates opened almost immediately, accelerated up the drive with obvious familiarity, Brail was prepared to bet that he was not a casual visitor, but either a member of the staff or Christopher Portman himself.

If it were Portman, he thought, it would be an interesting situation, and possibly profitable. But he would have to move carefully, wait and see what the police came up with, make a few painstaking inquiries.

He lingered further down the road for ten or fifteen minutes to make sure that the Toyota was not merely paying a brief visit to Charlbury Hall, then he rode on to Colombury. He was home in good time for tea. He ate with his wife; their two boys were out. His wife, Rita Brail, was a local girl and, except for a short period working in Reading where she had met Gavin, had lived in Colombury all her life, and thus was an excellent source of background information. Gavin wondered how he could broach the subject of Christopher Portman, and decided to come straight to the point – or more or less straight.

'The chaps at the garage were saying how many newcomers had moved into the district in the last ten years,' he said over his second cup. 'People like that rich man, Christopher Portman, who bought Charlbury Hall.'

'You can hardly call Portman a newcomer,' Rita objected. 'He was born in a cottage on Sir David Rocque's estate. His father was the head gardener at Wychwood Manor. He and Sir Bertram, who's now inherited the baronetcy, used to play together as children. Poor boy and rich boy.'

'Really? Well, the situation's changed, hasn't it? It's Portman who's the rich man and Rocque the poor. I don't suppose they're still friends.'

'Yes, they are, Gavin. Oh, I expect they lost touch while Portman was making his fortune, but they're friends again now.'

Rita gave one of her Mona Lisa smiles, but offered no more, and Brail thought it unwise to press her. It was better if she didn't suspect how interested he was. But he knew his wife, and knew that she had what she believed was some secret information, and sooner or later she would impart it to him. He could wait. Meanwhile, he yearned to have confirmation that the driver of the red Toyota had been Christopher Portman.

'I know Sir Bertram by sight,' he said. 'I've seen him in Colombury occasionally, but I don't know Portman at all. What does he look like?'

'Tall, dark and handsome!' Rita laughed. 'What with his looks and his money it's amazing he didn't get married years ago. Rumour has it that he keeps a mistress in London and –'

'And?'

'Lady Rocque is a very beautiful woman.'

'Rita!' Brail pretended to be shocked. 'You're a dreadful gossip.'

Rita laughed again. She was a pretty, rather simple girl, and didn't understand how full of guile her husband was. But if she could make him happy, she herself was happy, and she sensed that she had pleased him. It was fortunate for her that she couldn't read his thoughts at that moment.

Gavin Brail was thinking that if he played his cards right Christopher Portman might with a little persuasion prove an excellent investment.

While Portman and Brail each considered the possible consequences of the hit-and-run accident that had been responsible for Frankie Carton's death, Edmund Carton was still ignorant of the truth. But he was worried. He couldn't imagine why the boy was so late.

Edmund had been so immersed in a long article he was writing for *The Economist* that he hadn't noticed the time until he had suddenly felt hungry, and realized that he had done nothing about supper. He was horrified to discover how late it was. Where was Frankie? What had happened to him?

Once before, when the snow had been deep and Frankie had been forced to walk most of the way home, pushing his bike, he had been very late. But this was a fine day, not even raining. Edmund ran a hand through his thinning hair. Where on earth was the boy? What had kept him? He was always so reliable. Too reliable, Edmund thought. At his age Frankie should have been more unpredictable, more light-hearted, but with no mother and a father who loved him dearly, but since Margaret's death had become something of a recluse, he didn't have much of a life.

I must do more for him, Edmund thought. But how? Money was tight, tighter than he allowed Frankie to know, though he suspected that the boy guessed for Frankie never complained and often refused some small suggested treat.

Perhaps I should try to write more, Edmund mused, as he went down to the kitchen to put the casserole into the oven, but life as a freelance journalist wasn't easy. Perhaps he should never have given up his full-time job on *The Times*, but after Margaret's death he had been so depressed that he didn't care about anything or anyone, except Frankie. And Frankie had been so young then, only eight, that it had been difficult to look after him properly with a real job, and difficult to look ahead, to plan for the future.

Edmund went out of the small house a couple of miles outside Colombury that he had bought with his dead wife's money, and down the lane to the road. There was still no sign of Frankie, and by now he was seriously worried. Sighing, he returned to the house, a sad grey man, old beyond his years.

Reluctantly, because he knew Frankie didn't like him to phone Coriston College, he tapped out the school's number and asked for Mr Hauler; he knew Frankie was due to have a Latin coaching session that day. While waiting to be put through to the schoolmaster he watched out of the window, hoping to see Frankie ride up the lane.

'Hello! Jocelyn Hauler here.'

'Hello!' The voice had startled Edmund. 'This is Edmund Carton. I was wondering about Frankie. He's not home yet

22

and it – it's pretty late.' He cursed his stammer, which only occurred when he was under stress.

'He's not?' It was Hauler's turn to be startled. 'But he left the college hours ago. He should have been home long before this.'

'Well, he's not.'

There was silence on the line as the two men weighed the possibilities. They were both, in different ways, deeply concerned, but it was the younger who took the initiative.

'Mr Carton, I think you'd better stay at home. I'll get out my car and drive over to you. I'm bound to overtake Frankie. It's an obvious route to your house. I expect he's had a minor accident and damaged his bicycle in some fashion, and I'll find him carrying it. He wouldn't want to leave it by the wayside, would he?'

'No, I suppose not,' Edmund said doubtfully. 'Someone would probably nick it. All right, I'll wait here. It's very good of you.'

The police arrived first. Sergeant Donaldson had remained at the scene of the accident and had sent PC Wright and WPC Digby to the Cartons' house. They were both young and inexperienced and didn't relish their task, though Edmund made it relatively easy for them. He had seen an unmarked car come up the lane and, thinking it was Hauler, had come out to meet it. But the sight of the police uniforms prepared him.

'Mr Carton?' Wright asked.

'Yes. I'm Edmund Carton. It's my son, isn't it? He should have been home by now, but he isn't. Frankie's had an accident?'

'I'm afraid so, sir.'

'Perhaps we should go inside.' The WPC took Edmund by the arm and led him, unprotesting, back into the house. 'It's bad news, Mr Carton,' she said softly.

'How bad? Where is he? What's happened to him?'

'Your son is dead, Mr Carton. He was hit by a car and thrown on to the road. He died at once.' Wright lied gamely. 'He didn't suffer.'

Edmund didn't hear the lies. He was trying to absorb the fact that Frankie, his Frankie, Margaret's Frankie, was dead. And it was his fault. He ought never to have sent the boy to that damned school, made him cycle all those miles every day. He couldn't have saved Margaret. Everything had been done for her that could be done. But Frankie . . . Edmund collapsed into a chair and buried his face in his hands.

Wright watched him sympathetically. Digby went to find the kitchen and put on a kettle. They were glad when the doorbell rang and Jocelyn Hauler arrived. Hauler, who had come from the scene of the accident, had already learnt what had happened, and was pleased to see the police and to know that he didn't have to break the news to Frankie's father. He was badly shaken himself, but he knew that his own grief would have to wait.

As Wright led Hauler into the sitting-room and Digby brought in the tea, Edmund, his face streaked with tears, suddenly looked up. 'Who was it who killed Frankie? Was it a local man?'

'We don't know yet, sir,' Wright said. 'Your son wasn't able to help us.'

'Dear God!' Edmund said quite quietly. 'You find the bugger and I'll kill him.'

They were words that were to be remembered.

24

3

Edmund Carton put out his hand and turned off the alarm. The action woke him fully. He lay on his back in bed, and memory of the previous day hit him. Frankie was dead. Part of his mind protested that this wasn't true, that at any moment Frankie would come into the bedroom with their early morning tea. But he knew that it was a fact, and he groaned aloud.

He remembered the two police officers, their young faces furrowed with concern as they led him into the house, and their relief at the arrival of Hauler, as if Jocelyn Hauler had been a relation who could cope with the bereaved. And Hauler had coped. He had promised the officers he would take Edmund into Oxford the next day to identify the body of Francis Carton and deal with the formalities. He had cooked an omelette and forced Edmund to eat it. He had made more tea. He had found an unopened bottle of whisky. He had let Edmund talk, about his wife and his son, about his own childhood, about his early ambitions which Margaret's death had made immaterial, and about his life alone with Frankie. Presumably Hauler had, much later, put him to bed. He didn't remember that, but here he was in his shirt and underpants, covered by the duvet.

His instinct was to lie there, to feign sleep, to pretend that yesterday had never happened. But slowly he eased himself into a sitting position. A dull pain shot through his head and his stomach felt queasy, his mouth dry – obvious symptoms of a hangover – and he wondered how much whisky he had drunk the night before. Then, cautiously turning his head, he saw the note propped against the lamp on his bedside table and reached for it.

It read: *I have to go back to Coriston, but will pick you up tomorrow at ten. Hope that will be all right. I have set your alarm for eight. J.*

Bless Jocelyn Hauler, Edmund thought. Hauler had taken care of him the previous night, and now had given him two hours to wash and shave and prepare himself for the ordeal that lay ahead. He had done everything a friend could possibly do, and yet the man scarcely knew him.

But there was something Hauler hadn't done, Edmund thought – something that needed to be done. Beth, his sister, had to be told. Carefully, like a frail old man, he slid out of bed, put on a robe and, ignoring the pounding pain in his head, walked unsteadily along the passage to his workroom. He sat at his desk and tapped out Beth's number.

It was only a few minutes after eight, but he knew that his sister would be up and dressed. She didn't believe in pampering herself, or anyone else. She had often complained that he spoiled Frankie, which was absurd. Dear Frankie! Edmund ached for him, but he had no more tears to shed.

'Hello! Hello! Who is that?' Beth's well-known and somewhat imperious voice demanded.

'It's me, Edmund.' For a moment he was silent; he had suddenly found it impossible to continue.

'Edmund, my dear, what is it? What's wrong? Are you ill?'

Beth Randelson was full of concern. Twelve years older than Edmund, she had always been devoted to him. Left a young widow as a result of an industrial accident, compensation for which had provided her with a reasonable pension, she had opposed Edmund's marriage on the grounds of Margaret's poor health, but in fact she had been jealous of the beautiful semi-invalid, and the relationship between wife and sister-in-law had not been easy.

When Margaret had died, Beth had gladly offered a home to her brother and his eight-year-old son. To her annoyance, Edmund had refused to consider the suggestion. He had done so for Frankie's sake, fearing that Beth would prove to be too much of a martinet, and might unconsciously take out on the child her continuing resentment against Margaret.

'Edmund! Are you still there? Are you all right?' she asked again.

'Yes, I'm all right. It's not me, Beth. It's Frankie. He's been killed by some bloody hit-and-run driver.'

'Oh no! Oh, my poor Edmund! How dreadful for you. I'm so sorry, so very sorry.'

'I know. I really haven't taken it in yet. It just seems like a nightmare, quite unreal.'

'There'll be all sorts of practical matters to deal with. At least I can help you there, Edmund. I'll catch the night train. I'll be with you tomorrow, my dear.'

'Beth, I'm not sure –'

But Mrs Randelson wasn't prepared to listen. She did have a part-time job in her local public library, but they could easily do without her for a few days. Edmund was more important. Once again she assured him that she would be with him the next day, that she would take a taxi from the station and, if he had to go out, he was to leave the key to the back door under the mat.

There was no point in arguing with her. It was simpler to thank her and agree. And she would be of help, Edmund thought as he put down the receiver. He had no close friends, and he couldn't impose on Jocelyn Hauler indefinitely. He was lucky to have Beth.

While Edmund Carton forced himself to face the day, his first day without Frankie, Christopher Portman sat at his breakfast table reading the *Colombury Courier* instead of his usual *Financial Times*. If the choice surprised his secretary, Simon Wayne, the latter didn't comment. Wayne, who had been in Portman's employ for a dozen years and was by now his friend and confidant, knew that there were areas of Portman's life that he kept strictly private.

'More coffee, sir?' the houseman asked.

'Please,' Portman said absently, without looking up from the newspaper.

He reread the story. It contained an imaginary description

of Frankie's accident, a tirade against wild or drunk drivers who didn't care whom they killed, and a certain amount about the victim. It was this which interested Christopher Portman; Sergeant Donaldson's claim that the police were confident that the driver of the offending vehicle would soon be traced he didn't really believe.

He didn't learn much from the paper about Francis Carton, merely his name, age, the fact that he was the only child of Edmund Carton, a widower, that he had won a scholarship to Coriston, that he planned to go to Oxford – information provided by Hauler, who had kept the reporter away from Edmund. But it was enough for Portman to conjure up a picture of the boy, and he assumed there would be more details in the next edition of the *Courier*, in the *Oxford Mail* and possibly in the national press. Meanwhile, there was nothing to be done but wait. It would be unwise to make inquiries about Edmund Carton at the moment. Perhaps later, when the boy's death was no longer news, he might be able to do the father a good turn, help him in some way – a salve to his own conscience, he thought bitterly.

Suddenly aware that he had been staring at the same page of the *Courier* for several minutes and that Wayne had been watching him curiously, Portman folded up the local paper and picked up the *Financial Times*. For a split second he had been tempted to tell Wayne the truth about the accident, but it was a temptation he instantly suppressed, for it would have been unfair to burden his secretary with the knowledge.

Instead he said, 'I borrowed Bertram Rocque's car yesterday. I'll have to return it this morning. Would you follow me to the Manor? Then I thought we might go straight to the club and have a round of golf.'

'That sounds an excellent idea,' Wayne said, and told himself that there was nothing wrong, that he had imagined Christopher had seen an item in the *Courier* that worried him. 'It'll help blow away the cobwebs.' He hoped this wasn't an unfortunate choice of phrase.

Gavin Brail had also read the story in the *Courier*, but once he had learnt the identity of the victim he was not particularly

28

interested in further details. He had met Edmund Carton, who had brought his old motorbike into the Windrush Garage some months ago – he was not happy about the brakes and Gavin had done his best to repair the trouble, though he had pointed out that the bike was way past its prime. He remembered that Carton had said he was quite aware of that and, if he had to replace it, he might go for an inexpensive second-hand car. So the father of Francis Carton was a poor man – unlike the owner of Charlbury Hall.

Brail worked on alternate Saturdays, and it so happened that the day after Frankie was killed he was free. He kicked a football around the small back garden of their council house, did a little carpentry and went into the town to do some shopping for Rita. The shopping done, he decided to have a pint at the Windrush Arms in the hope of hearing any gossip about the accident.

He was in luck, PC Wright, off duty, was in the bar and happy to talk. From Wright, Brail learnt that the approximate time of Frankie's death had been established, because it was known when he left Coriston. But this hadn't helped the police much, as so far no car had been identified on that stretch of road at that time. Nor was there any other evidence. There had been no give-away skid marks, and only a scrape of red paint on the remains of the bicycle to suggest that the boy had been hit by a red vehicle.

'There are hundreds – thousands – of red cars or vans on the roads,' Wright said. 'A sliver of red paint means very little. I know how paints can be identified and matched by Forensic, but we can't examine every red vehicle in the area trying to find something to match the sliver. Personally, I don't believe we'll ever catch the blighter who was driving, unless he has a crisis of conscience and owns up.'

'And what are the chances of that?' someone asked.

'Not great,' Wright said.

Brail would have put it more strongly. If it had been Portman driving the Toyota – and that was far from being a hundred per cent certain as yet – Brail considered it most improbable that he would admit his guilt. While secretly envying them, Gavin Brail had a low opinion of the moral behaviour of men like Christopher Portman, who had made their own fortunes.

'Will you just drop the case then?' he asked.

'Stop making our inquiries, you mean? Officially, no. But what do you think, chum?' Wright grinned at Brail. 'We're busy people, you know. It may not be a crime every second in these parts, but we have more than enough to do.'

'I bet,' Brail said, implying admiration, though he had no particular liking for the local police.

Wright was looking suggestively at his empty tankard and Brail decided it was time he went home; he wasn't in the business of buying pints for the fuzz. Outside the Windrush Arms, he looked up and down the street, and noted that three of the parked cars were red. It was a moment before he took in the fact that the one directly opposite the pub was a Toyota.

He strolled across the street and looked in the nearest shop window, pretending to study the men's clothing on display, while he watched the car behind him. He had already seen the licence plate and knew that this was the Toyota which he had followed to Charlbury Hall, and which he believed had killed Frankie Carton.

As he watched, a woman came out of the butcher's. She put her package on the back seat of the Toyota and got into the front, but not behind the wheel. She was in her mid-to late-thirties, Brail reckoned, a slim woman with light brown hair, bleached by the sun and wind, and a long, tired-looking face. She was not unattractive, but he would not have called her beautiful, not by his standards, not by the standards of film stars or presenters on the telly, and Brail couldn't imagine her as the wife of Sir Bertram Rocque – and a mistress, as Rita had suggested, of Christopher Portman.

But almost at once the question of her identity was answered. A man came hurrying along the street and got into the Toyota beside her. Seen together, dressed in similar elderly tweed suits, the resemblance between them was strong, and Brail had recognized Sir Bertram Rocque. The woman was obviously the sister, who lived with him.

'I saw the Rocques shopping in Colombury this morning,' Brail remarked ingenuously when he got home.

Rita didn't disappoint him; she was ready to gossip. 'Well, don't you think she's beautiful? She was an actress, you know, before she married him.'

'You're talking about the wife. I meant the sister, Miss Rocque.'

'Oh, she's not Miss Rocque. She's a Mrs – Mrs Mariner. She married young, still in her teens, and the marriage didn't last. She was back home again inside a year. There were all sorts of rumours, that he beat her and was unfaithful, and that he really preferred boys. No one knew the truth. Anyway, there was a divorce and she's lived at the Manor ever since. She helps her brother run the place. In fact, he'd probably have gone bankrupt without her. He's a nice easy-going chap, but not much of a businessman.'

'Does the wife help too?'

'With the market garden? I shouldn't think so.' Rita laughed. 'She's just decorative. I don't expect Daphne – Mrs Mariner – was any too pleased when he married her. She must have believed Bertram was a confirmed bachelor, and she'd always be the lady of the manor.'

'Disappointing for her,' Brail said, but he had lost interest in Daphne Mariner; it was the red Toyota, which presumably Portman had borrowed, that intrigued him. 'Incidentally, how do you know all this?'

'Just casual conversation at the hairdresser's,' said Rita mildly.

On Monday morning, Brail asked Mr Field – the owner, and his boss – where the people from the big houses in the district bought their cars if it was not from the Windrush Garage.

'Thinking of drumming up some business for us?' Field asked.

Brail shrugged. 'I saw Sir Bertram Rocque's Toyota in town on Saturday, and it occurred to me he never brings it in here.'

'No. He uses a small garage in Little Chipping. I expect he finds it cheaper.'

Brail registered that Rocque's shortage of money seemed to be common knowledge, and accepted as more than mere relative poverty. 'What about Mr Portman at Charlbury Hall?' he asked.

'Now there's someone whose business I'd like to have,' Field admitted. 'He's got some fine cars, including a Roller and a Ferrari. But he's also got a chauffeur who's a skilled mechanic. I do occasionally supply a part, but I believe any big jobs are done in London.'

A customer interrupted them, but Brail had run out of questions for the garage proprietor. What next, he wondered, as he went about his day's work? It was a fair assumption that the Toyota belonged to Rocque, but he had seen Portman – if it was Portman – driving the damned car. Of course, he could forget the whole thing, but in that case he'd have no hope of cashing in on it.

No, he couldn't give up such a golden opportunity. He would have to find out for certain if it was Portman who had been driving the Toyota, and there was only one reliable way to do that. Ask the man himself.

After work, Brail went along to the railway station where he could use a public telephone box. He had looked up the numbers of Charlbury Hall – there were three – at the garage, and had been glad to find them listed. He had planned what he intended to say, but he was nervous and when a woman's voice – presumably that of a maid – answered, 'Charlbury Hall', he nearly put down the receiver.

'I would like to speak to Mr Portman, please. This is the police.'

'One moment, sir.'

While he waited he could feel his heart thumping and again he was tempted to abandon the whole enterprise. He told himself he would count to ten, and if no one had answered by then . . . But he had only reached seven when a different – male – voice announced that Mr Portman's secretary was speaking.

'I would like to speak to Mr Portman personally, please.' Brail did his best to sound official. 'It's a police inquiry in connection with that accident on Friday when Francis Carton, the boy from Coriston, was killed.'

'I'll see if Mr Portman is available,' the voice said unpromisingly.

There was another wait, and then another voice, which Brail immediately associated with the driver of the Toyota, came on the line. To his surprise, his nervousness had disappeared. He felt in control of the situation.

'I'm sorry to bother you, sir,' he said. 'Police Constable Grant here. It's in connection with that accident on Friday. My colleague who stopped your Toyota and helped you to back up and take a diversion forgot to ask if you had seen any other vehicles on the road.'

'No, Officer, I didn't, but then I had only come from Wychwood Manor.'

'What about when you were going the opposite way, sir, to Sir Bertram's house?'

'No-o. I'm afraid I can't help you there either. The car or whatever it was that hit the boy must have been behind me.'

'Well, thank you very much, sir. I'm sorry to have bothered you.'

'That's all right, Officer. I hope you find whoever did it.'

'I bet,' said Brail to himself as he replaced the receiver and, jubilant at what he had learnt, set off home.

4

Ten days passed. They were days of grief for Edmund Carton, consoled by his sister Beth, to whom he left all practical matters while he lived in a haze. They were days of grief, too, and of slowly diminishing shock, for Jocelyn Hauler, made worse by the fact that he had to hide his special feelings; the grief and the shock were of course shared by the staff and by many of the pupils at Coriston.

For Christopher Portman, they were days of worry, which affected those close to him, and especially his secretary, Simon Wayne, his mistress, Andrea Rocque, and Daphne Mariner, who was in love with him; Bertram Rocque seemed not to notice how tense Christopher had become, but Bertram had his own anxieties.

For Gavin Brail, they were days of anticipation. Mostly he was happy, with the nervous happiness of a man who has put his shirt on a dead cert for the Derby, but nevertheless fears that someone will nobble the horse before the great day. He spent a lot of time planning how he would deal with Portman, and even more dreaming about what he would do with his winnings when he got them. But he did have an occasional nightmare. After all, though he had often cheated and thieved in the past, he had never before tried his hand at blackmail, at least not on this scale. Once or twice he might have twisted the arm of a fellow worker, but this was different. This was the big time – his big chance.

Brail waited out the ten days impatiently. He waited this length of time because he reckoned that if by then the police hadn't found the driver of the red Toyota, they never would. Moreover, Portman would have begun to feel safe, and it would be a greater blow to him to discover that his secret was no longer secure. In Brail's judgement, this would be the moment to put his plan into action.

So, once again Brail went to the railway station after work and telephoned Charlbury Hall. He hoped Portman wouldn't be away, but was reassured when the same procedure as before was followed, and Portman eventually came on the line. Now, Brail was confident, particularly since he hadn't been asked to state his business, but had merely given the secretary the name of Police Constable Grant – a name he was sure Portman would recognize from his earlier phone call.

'Mr Portman,' he began, 'have you checked on the identity of PC Grant with the Colombury police station?'

'No. Should I have done?'

Portman sounded surprised, but recognized trouble immediately, for in spite of the delay he had been half-expecting further developments. It had occurred to him at the time of the first call that he might check on Grant, but the man had known what he was talking about and Portman had told himself that he had probably imagined there was something odd about the call; anyway, he had decided that it would be wiser not to demonstrate any particular interest and to take no action. Now, thanking God he was alone in his office, he switched on the recorder attached to his phone.

'It might have been wiser, Mr Portman. At least you would have learnt that there is no such officer.'

'What do you want?' Portman was blunt.

'To do a little business with you. But I must begin by giving you some information, Mr Portman. On the Friday afternoon that Francis Carton was killed, a red Toyota was seen driving along that stretch of road. It had already narrowly missed knocking down and possibly killing or maiming a motorcyclist. The car belongs to Sir Bertram Rocque of Wychwood Manor, but you were the driver, Mr Portman. You killed young Frankie.'

There was a short pause, then Portman said evenly, 'Even assuming that what you say is correct, it would be your word against mine, and why should anyone believe you? You have no evidence.'

'That is the rest of the information I intend to give you, Mr Portman. The police know it was a red car. Paint was found on Frankie's bike. When this is analysed by the experts in Oxford, they'll know it came from a Toyota. Of course there are hundreds of red Toyotas around – probably thousands – and there's no reason to suppose that Frankie was killed by someone local. Moreover, Sir Bertram Rocque is an important man. The police would think twice before they impounded his car unless – unless, Mr Portman, they were given cause to believe it was the vehicle that had brought about the boy's death – the licence number, say.'

'And you propose to give them such cause unless – unless, Mr Blackmailer, I buy your silence. Is that it?'

'Yes, that's it. How clever of you to work it out so quickly, Mr Portman. But then you must be a clever man to have made such a large fortune.'

Not clever enough by half, Portman thought. He remembered the Toyota overtaking a motorbike and causing it to swerve. But, as he visualized the scene again, he couldn't believe the rider had been quick and smart enough to correct the swerve, take in the make of the car and read its number plate. No, it had been later, when he had been on his way back from the Manor. The man had drawn up beside him while he was speaking to the police officer, had recognized the car and had followed him. It was bad luck – incredibly bad luck – and his own damned fault.

He should have left the Rocques' car and walked home, or at least avoided the scene of the accident, but he had felt a need to return there as soon as possible to make sure that, even after this delay, there was nothing he could do for the boy.

'How much, Mr Blackmailer?' he demanded.

'Don't call me that!'

'Why not? It's what you are, isn't it?'

'No. I'm offering you a simple business proposition. If you don't want to take part in it I'll go to the police, and you'll go to prison.'

'Where I might be sharing a cell with you,' Portman said. 'Attempted blackmail is a serious crime, you know. Juries don't like it.'

But as soon as he had spoken, Portman knew it was a useless threat. The tape recording of their present conversation could be damning, but he had no idea who the blackmailer was. The man beside him at that crucial time had taken off his crash helmet in order to hear what he and the policeman had been saying, but he had scarcely glanced at him, and would be incapable of identifying him.

'Mr Portman, you're in no position to bargain. Be sensible! I want a hundred thousand pounds, that's all, and that'll be the end of it. I'm not asking for the moon. A hundred grand, and it's worth it to you. You're a rich man. You won't notice the money.'

A hundred thousand pounds. It was true, Portman thought, it was not a vast sum. He could easily afford it. But it would not be all, whatever the man claimed. Even if he meant it now, the temptation to come to the well for more would be too great for him, and anyway the idea of submitting to blackmail was anathema. Nevertheless, for the moment he had no choice; he would have to play along.

'OK, you win. A hundred thousand – but no more.'

'Agreed.' Brail couldn't keep the triumph from his voice.

'How do you want it and how do I get it to you? I assume you won't accept a cheque through the mail.'

Brail laughed. He wouldn't have laughed if he could have seen Portman's face. Christopher Portman hadn't got where he was through weakness and a refusal to take risks. Besides, he was an experienced negotiator with more or less unlimited resources. He wasn't going to be beaten so easily.

'No, I don't want a cheque, Mr Portman. I want the money in notes, used notes, varied denominations, and don't try any clever tricks like attempting to trace me through the serial numbers, or you'll be sorry.' Brail was feeling even more sure of himself. 'You understand?'

'I understand,' Portman said, and added to himself, more than you think I understand. Even from this phone call I've learnt more about you than you would believe, and I'll put my knowledge to good use. In my book, blackmailers don't deserve pity. Then aloud, 'Mr – er – Grant,' he continued, 'I must call you by some name. As you say, I'm a rich man, but I do not keep a hundred thousand pounds lying around the house. Most of my money is tied up, and I shall have to be careful how I assemble that sum in used notes without arousing suspicion. It will take me a couple of weeks to organize.'

'One week!' Brail was confident that he was now in full control of the situation.

'Very well. One week,' Portman said with seeming reluctance. 'How do I get it to you?'

Brail had considered this problem carefully, aware that it covered the moment when he would be most vulnerable. 'Make up the money in a parcel and put it in a carrier bag. There's a rubbish bin beside the games pavilion on the Colombury sports ground. You know where I mean?'

'I can find it.'

'Right. Put the bag in the bin this day next week at seven in the evening and buzz off at once. Come alone, Mr Portman. If I see any suspicious characters in the vicinity I won't collect it, and you know what will happen to you then.'

'You watch too much television, Mr Grant.'

'What? Just do as I say! Have you understood?'

'Yes. Do I have your word this will be the end of the matter?'

'You do, Mr Portman.'

You bloody liar, Christopher Portman thought, and he replaced his receiver very gently.

Christopher Portman was playing back his conversation with Brail when there was a gentle tap on the door and Simon Wayne came into the room, a sheaf of papers in his hand. Portman instinctively switched off the recorder.

'Sorry, I didn't know you were busy,' Wayne said. 'I'll come back later. There's a rumour that the yen is about to be devalued. It probably isn't true, but the markets are jittery and we do hold rather a lot of Namikura stock.'

Portman looked at him. He had heard the words, but they

38

had had no meaning. He couldn't think of stocks and shares and currencies and rates of exchange at the moment. His mind was focused on the man he called Grant, and his thoughts were grim.

'Chris, are you all right?'

'No, not really, Simon.' Portman had changed his mind. He hadn't wanted to involve Wayne, but he couldn't deal with Grant by himself. He badly needed help, which meant that he would have to trust someone, and there was no one on whom he could depend more than Simon Wayne. 'Come and sit down. I want you to listen to this recording of a telephone conversation I had a short while ago.'

Wayne sat, still clutching his papers, and waited for the bad news. He had rarely seen Christopher Portman so on edge. Portman switched on the recording and Wayne listened with increasing distress and horror, which he did his best not to show. He failed.

'You're appalled, aren't you, Simon? You were in London at the time, but you read about this accident and you must have thought what a shit the driver was not to stop?'

'Yes, Chris, I did.' Wayne didn't elaborate.

Portman's smile was wry. 'At least you're honest, Simon.'

'What did you expect me to say?' Wayne was suddenly angry. 'That tape is – is bad news. You're in trouble, Chris, dire trouble, and I don't understand how it happened. Why didn't you stop? It's just not like you. I remember once when we were in France you killed a cat. It wasn't your fault. You couldn't have avoided the wretched animal. But you stopped and insisted on finding the owner and over-compensating him. And that was only for a mangy tabby, not a child!'

Wayne stopped, his anger evaporating as quickly as it had come. Now there remained only concern for Christopher Portman. 'Chris, this is serious. You could go to prison for years. In God's name, how did it happen? It's so – unlike you,' he repeated. 'You're one of the most caring, generous people I know.'

'Thanks!'

'I mean it, Chris. How did it happen? How on earth did

you get yourself into this mess? Why were you driving Bertram's car anyway?'

'Simon, before I explain — and I'll try to explain to your satisfaction — I'd like you to answer two questions.'

'All right, Chris.' Wayne was impatient. 'What are they?'

'First, if you want no part in this affair, which I would quite understand, will you swear that whatever the circumstances you will never reveal or hint at what I'm about to tell you?'

'You mean, if it comes to it, I should let you go to the gallows, as it were?' Simon Wayne shook his head. 'OK, Chris, if that's your wish. I swear.'

'Secondly, will you help me to get out of the mess I'm in, even if doing so entails breaking the law?'

'That requires no thought,' Wayne said instantly. 'Of course I'll do anything I can to help. You didn't need to ask that.'

'Thanks.' For a long minute Portman was silent, then he said, 'It's really quite simple. It all started with an invitation to the Sinclair–Jowett wedding in Chipping Norton. The Sinclairs are great friends of Andrea Rocque's. Bertram refused to go on the grounds that he was too busy, and Daphne Mariner agreed with him. To be honest, they don't like the Sinclairs, who are a rather brash lot, though quite harmless, but as you know, the one thing you can't do to Bertram is to appear to patronize him. Anyhow, I'd also been invited to the wedding and I said I would escort Andrea and pick her up, but Bertram, who was feeling particularly touchy that day, insisted that Andrea should pick me up as my house was on the way from the Manor to Chipping Norton. That, in fact, is not quite true, and in any case there was only a couple of miles in it. But I acquiesced. And that, Simon, was my first mistake.'

'It explains why you didn't have one of your own cars.'

'Yes, it does that of course. Well, the wedding was like most weddings, lots of champagne and false jollity and snide remarks about how long the marriage would last. It was the second time round for both of them. I wished I hadn't come — I probably would have cried off at the last moment if I

40

hadn't been committed to Andrea – and I was thankful when it was time to go.'

'How much had you drunk, Chris?'

Portman laughed. 'Three glasses of champagne. But you'll have to take my word for that, Simon. I'm damned sure no one else will vouch for it.'

'And if anyone did, no judge or jury would believe him.'

'I was careful what I drank because I expected to drive, but Andrea beat me to the driving seat. I couldn't face a scene in front of our hosts and all the other retreating guests, so I didn't argue, but as soon as we were on our own I suggested I should take over, though I admit she wasn't driving badly – just slightly erratically. But the suggestion made her furious. We had a row. At one point she stopped the car and told me I could get out and walk home. I should have done just that; to refuse was my second mistake. Andrea began to drive faster and faster and more and more carelessly. I was holding my breath, waiting for us to have an accident. She swept past the turning that would have led us here to the Hall and then, suddenly, we came around a corner and ploughed into the boy on his bicycle.

'Simon, I tried to make her stop. We struggled over the wheel. Twice we nearly went into a stone wall. I thought she was going to kill us both. By this time she was completely irresponsible – I hadn't realized how tight she was – and she was driving like a maniac. Eventually we rocketed up the drive to the Manor. God knows how we managed to get through the gateway.

'I had intended to bundle her out and drive back to where we had hit the boy, but by now she'd collapsed. I had to find Alice, and I helped her get Andrea upstairs to her room. I told her Lady Rocque had been taken ill, but she knew that was a lie. All this took time. I was sure that by then the boy would have been found. There had been a motorcyclist we had overtaken – the chap who's trying to blackmail me, I guess.

'I took the Toyota to get home; I hesitated at the end of Wychwood Manor's drive. By turning right and making a slight detour I could reach the Hall without passing the accident. But I needed to know what had happened to the boy, so I turned left and returned to the scene of the crime, as the police will probably call it. That was my final mistake. In fact, the police were in control; they had closed the road to take measurements or something, and an officer stopped me to tell me so and ask me to back up and make a detour; the detour, in fact, was the one I had thought about taking, and led right past the Manor. It was while I was talking to the officer that the motorcyclist caught up with me again. He followed me to the Hall on his bike, and must have discovered who I was. And that's the whole sorry story, Simon.'

Simon Wayne nodded. It was both better and worse than he had expected. He was thankful that the high opinion of Chris Portman that he'd always held had not been dented, but he was even more fearful for his friend.

'Chris, I have to ask you. Obviously Grant – or whatever his name is – believes you were driving when the boy was killed, but Andrea knows this isn't true. What has she to say about the accident?'

'She – er – she says she can't remember anything at all about it. She says she remembers feeling horribly ill and being helped out of the car, but she doesn't remember driving at any time on the way home from the wedding.'

'What? For God's sake, Chris, you can't believe her.'

Portman shrugged. 'She hasn't denied being responsible for the boy's death. She hasn't accused me. She merely claims to have had a blackout, so that her mind's a blank over that period.'

'The bitch! The utter bitch!' Wayne muttered. Then he had a thought. 'But, Chris, some of the wedding guests must have seen that she was driving, not you, when you left the Sinclairs.'

'We could have stopped – as I tried to do – and changed places. Simon, it's no use. Can you see me standing in the dock and saying, ''I am not guilty. It was Lady Rocque who killed the boy''? Even if anyone believed me, I couldn't bring myself to point the finger at her, for Bertram's sake if nothing else.'

'She seems quite prepared to let *you* take the blame.'

'I suspect she's hoping the police will get nowhere, and the matter will be forgotten. She doesn't know about the blackmailer, and I don't intend to tell her. No, there's only one way to deal with the situation, other than pay blackmail – a course I refuse to consider.'

'And what's that?'

'To persuade the bloody man to keep his mouth shut.'

'How do you propose to achieve that?'

'By frightening him half to death. I know it sounds mad. I know it may not work. But I got the impression from what he said that he sees things in terms of TV drama, and I was hoping we might lay on an episode for him, an episode he won't enjoy, so that he'll be too scared after it to take any action against me.'

'It's an awful risk. It may make him dash off to the police and the media – the reverse of what you want.'

'I know. But I shan't be any worse off than if he does that now. I think it's a risk worth taking. Of course, if you've any better suggestion, Simon –'

'No.'

It was a lie. If Simon Wayne had had his way he would have forced Andrea Rocque to confess, if necessary bluffing her that she had been seen by a man on a motorbike, and it would be much worse for her if the chap went to the police first. But he knew it would be useless to propose this. Christopher would never agree.

'We'll do as you say, Chris,' he said, and added to himself, 'And just pray it will work, whatever "it" is.'

5

Gavin Brail was cock-a-hoop. The thought of the hundred thousand pounds soon to be his filled him with elation. In his mind he was already spending it. His only doubt was whether he had asked enough, but he realized that he could always come back for more. It was best not to appear too greedy at the outset. After all, once Portman had paid he would have admitted his guilt, and would be in no position to make any bargains.

As the big day grew slowly nearer, Brail couldn't contain his anticipation. He whistled at his work, until someone asked him if he had won the pools. He laughed off the joke, but when Rita asked him why he was so cheerful he hesitated. He yearned to tell her, but knew he mustn't. Rita could be surprisingly high minded on occasion. But he couldn't resist the temptation to hint.

'How would you feel about leaving Colombury and going to live in a big city, love?' he asked.

'You mean Oxford?'

'No. You'd always be popping home to mother if we lived in Oxford. Besides, apart from the university, Oxford's not much of a town. I was thinking more of Birmingham or Glasgow or even –'

'I wouldn't mind Bristol.'

'Now that *is* an idea!'

Rita had an elder sister who had married and gone to live in Bristol, so they would have family there and she wouldn't be lonely. Besides, he liked Bristol. He pictured a little house on the outskirts and his own business, not unlike the Windrush Garage, but bigger and more lucrative.

'Yes,' he said, 'Bristol would suit us just fine.'

'But Gavin – I don't understand. Why should we be thinking of leaving Colombury?'

'We can't stay here all our lives, Rita. I've got ambitions, and I can't get any further at Field's place. There's no hope of a partnership. He's got a son.'

'A partnership?' Rita was round-eyed at the idea.

'Why not? You'd like a bigger house, wouldn't you? And when the boys grow a bit older and start bringing girls home, they'll want a place to be proud of.' Suddenly Brail was overcome by caution. 'I've plans, see, for the four of us, but don't you go spoiling them with a lot of gossip – not even to your family. Understand?'

'I understand,' said Rita Brail, and thought what a wonderful husband Gavin was.

She too began to dream dreams of what might be in store for them, but, fortunately, for once she kept her mouth shut, and she didn't have long to wait for further news. Brail had given Portman only a week to assemble the money and, though the time seemed to Brail to pass exceedingly slowly, if pleasurably, the day he was anticipating soon arrived.

It was a cold, raw day with a threat of rain in the wind. At ten minutes to six, when Gavin Brail was thinking of clearing his tools and washing up after his work, so that he could go home for a quick tea and allow himself plenty of time to get to the playing field and his rendezvous with Christopher Portman's money, one of the Windrush Garage's regular customers brought in his car.

Normally, Brail wouldn't have minded doing a half-hour's overtime, but this evening was different. He thought of refusing, but decided it might be unwise, or even suspicious. He phoned Rita to tell her he had a job to do and would be late home, then set to work on the car.

It took him longer than he had estimated and he realized that he would have no time to go home before meeting Portman. In fact, he arrived at the playing field with only a few minutes to spare. In spite of the cold, he was sweating. He waited impatiently, eager for this part of the operation to be over and to be on his way, the money safely in his possession.

Portman was late. As the minutes passed and he still hadn't appeared, Brail became angry. Portman had agreed to pay. If he didn't, he'd go to prison, but that would be no consolation for the loss of the money.

Then, when Brail had almost given up hope, a tall figure appeared. He was wearing a duffel coat, its hood pulled well down over his face to give protection against the rain, which was now steady. The figure hesitated for a second under a lamp post, so that Brail was able to see the carrier bag. Then he strode to the nearby rubbish bin, deposited the bag, turned and hurried away.

Brail sighed with relief. Apart from being a little late, Portman had obeyed instructions to the letter.

Jubilantly, Brail made himself count to fifty before he walked at an unhurried pace to the rubbish bin and extracted the carrier bag. It felt pleasantly heavy, and his spirits soared yet further. He couldn't examine the contents here, but he wanted to shout aloud in his excitement and triumph. He had won! He had bested the clever rich bastard! He had got a hundred thousand smackers! Now he too was rich, and he promised himself he was soon going to be richer.

His jubilation was short-lived. One moment he was alone, rejoicing in what he believed he had achieved, and the next moment two large figures had loomed up out of the darkness, one on either side of him. He was seized under the armpits and was being propelled along the path before he had fully taken in what was happening, but instinctively he hung on to the carrier bag, clutching it to his chest.

'What the fucking hell? What are you doing? Who the hell are you?' he managed to gasp.

The men didn't answer. Brail turned his head from one to the other, but they had passed the lamp post and were in deep shadow, so that all he could see were tall dark shapes. He started to struggle, but immediately the grips on him tightened, his feet were kicked from under him, and he was literally carried along. He still clung to the carrier bag.

By now they had reached the road where he had left his

motorbike, but it was no longer there. Instead, a small van stood by the kerb, its rear doors open, and he glimpsed his bike inside. Then he felt himself lifted and flung into the interior beside the bike. The two men followed him, the doors were shut and, in response to a slap on the metal panel separating them from the driver, the van moved off. Brail was sick with fear.

They drove for some distance. Lying on the floor of the vehicle, Brail had no sense of direction, and therefore no idea where they might be going, but he knew when they left the road and bounced over rough ground.

Suddenly, the van stopped. A light went on inside and for the first time he was able to get a good look at his captors. It was no help. They were both identically dressed in black, and wore black Balaclava helmets.

One of them bent over him, took off his crash helmet and started to search his pockets. When the carrier bag got in his way, he wrenched it from Brail's grasp, but left it beside him. He studied Brail's notebook, his driving licence and the contents of his wallet; the photograph of Rita and the two boys seemed to be of particular interest to him.

'You see, you've made a mistake,' Brail said eagerly. 'I'm not the chap you want. I'm just a motor mechanic, not anyone important. I work at the Windrush Garage.'

The man hit him across the face, first one way, then the other, jarring his teeth and making his head ring. 'No mistake, blackmailer.'

Brail's heart sank. The word blackmailer had told him everything he didn't want to know. Mr Christopher Portman was behind his abduction or whatever it was, and was responsible for his present plight. He'd been a fool. He had underestimated Portman, and now he was in terrible trouble. What were they planning to do with him? How far would Portman go? Would they kill him? At the very thought he began to whimper.

'Shut up!' the man said, replacing his notebook, driving licence and wallet. 'We're not going to kill you – not this time, not if you're a good little man.'

'What do you want? I'll do anything you like, anything.'

'We intend to put you to sleep, blackmailer, and – '

'But you said you weren't going to – to – ' Brail felt the front of his trousers grow wet and warm as, in his terror, he failed to control his bladder.

'When you wake up you will have forgotten you ever attempted to blackmail Mr Portman about anything; you'll have forgotten that you ever spoke to Mr Portman on the phone or anywhere else. Do you understand? The whole incident will have been completely erased from your mind.'

'I understand. I promise. I've forgotten already.'

'Let it remain that way.'

'Is that all? I can go?'

'Not quite all, Mr Gavin Brail. You've committed a crime and you must pay for it, so that you know we are serious, and know that if you break that promise you've made us you'll regret it bitterly.'

'But – but how can I pay?'

'You'll see. It has been arranged.' To Brail's ears, the words sounded ominous.

The second man, who so far hadn't spoken, got to his feet and tapped on the panel behind the driver. 'Five minutes,' he said.

Brail sweated. He didn't dare ask what was to happen in five minutes and luckily for him he didn't have to wait all that time. Only a few seconds passed before a pad suddenly covered his nose and mouth and he felt himself sinking into unconsciousness. He struggled desperately, believing that he had been told lies and that he was about to die. But it was a brief struggle.

Five minutes later when the van moved off, Gavin Brail was snoring peacefully.

Christopher Portman was dining with friends at the Garrick Club. He had been driven up to London that morning in the Rolls and had spent a busy day in the City. Now, outwardly, he was completely relaxed, enjoying good food and wine in pleasant company. Only someone who knew him very well would have appreciated how tense he was, and what an effort it was costing him to behave normally and avoid showing his anxiety.

However, as the evening progressed, it required yet more effort to concentrate on the conversation around him and not to let his mind wander on to what might be happening in Colombury. He wished he could have been there, taking part, sharing the risks, but Simon Wayne had been adamant; if necessary, Chris had to be able to prove that he had been nowhere near the scene of action, so that if anything went wrong no blame could be attached to him.

The plan they had devised was simple. Wayne would recruit two young men in London, brothers known to him who, as it happened, owed Portman a favour, and arrange for them to hire a van. They were completely trustworthy and would almost certainly look on it as an adventure. Nevertheless, they would be told the minimum, merely that a villain was trying to blackmail Portman, who didn't wish to go to the police because a lady was involved. The brothers would pick up Wayne at the gates of Charlbury Hall and drive him to the rendezvous. Wayne would take Portman's place, delivering a carrier bag which appeared to contain the money, and would then take over driving the van, while the brothers dealt with the would-be blackmailer.

There was no reason why anything should go wrong, but the unexpected could always happen. A chance passer-by, a man walking his dog, might see something suspicious and inform the police. It was even possible that the van might break down.

'Yes, indeed. I agree. It's a splendid show,' Portman said to the woman on his right who had addressed him; he had no idea what she had been talking about, though his response had apparently been reasonably apt.

Nevertheless, 'You're very distrait this evening, Christopher,' his neighbour said reproachfully.

'I'm sorry,' he apologized. 'I've had a trying day, and I'm rather exhausted.'

She patted him on the hand. 'You work too hard,' she said. 'You're always on duty.'

As if to prove her right, a waiter appeared at Portman's

elbow. 'There's a telephone call for you, sir. Will you take it in the booth, or shall I bring a phone to the table?'

'In the booth. Then I won't disturb my friends,' Portman said hastily, excusing himself.

He followed the waiter to a booth outside the dining-room and waited for the call to be put through. He was surprised how nervous he felt. It was a relief to hear Wayne's voice.

'Our business went exactly according to plan, Chris. No alarms. It couldn't have been simpler.'

'That's splendid. You're home again now?'

'Yes, I'm fine. The boys dropped me at the end of the drive. They'll return the van in the morning. I gave them each a little extra present as you suggested, and they said to tell you they're at your service at any time.'

'I hope that won't be necessary,' Portman said shortly. 'Simon, they weren't too rough, were they?'

'No. I warned them, and I'm sure they did only what was required.'

'Good. See you tomorrow then, and you can fill in the blanks. And thanks, Simon – more than I can say.'

'No need.'

Portman put down the receiver. The mental response to his relief made him lean against the side of the booth for a few moments. So far everything had gone well, it appeared. Whatever happened next, Simon and the boys should be in the clear. He would lie, if necessary commit perjury, to protect them, but with luck the occasion wouldn't arise. Everything depended on the reaction of the blackmailer. Had he been cowed, as they hoped and, Portman reminded himself, as the man deserved, or would he immediately seek revenge? It was wait-and-see time again.

Christopher Portman gritted his teeth, left the booth and returned to the dining-room. He apologized profusely, blaming business affairs and concentrated on being the perfect guest for the rest of the evening.

As soon as he had finished speaking to Portman, Simon tapped out the number of the Colombury police station.

'I've just passed what seems to be an accident on the road

50

between Colombury and Little Chipping,' he said. 'A motor-cyclist has driven into one of the stone walls you have in these parts. He's alive but unconscious and I think an ambulance should get there as soon as possible. As far as I could tell the place is – '

'Yes. Thank you, sir. We know. It's already been reported and an ambulance and a police car are on their way. May I have your name, please?'

Wayne put down the receiver without answering. He wished he hadn't phoned, but Portman had insisted that the man shouldn't be left lying on the grass verge for too long, especially as the forecast had been for a cold, wet night. But it wouldn't matter, Wayne thought. It wasn't unusual in the circumstances for a driver who had assured himself there was nothing he could do, not to stay at the scene of the accident, and he had implied that he was a stranger.

Wayne poured himself a stiff whisky and turned on the television set. He was restless. Like Portman, he wasn't looking forward to the waiting period they both knew must inevitably follow the night's events.

The police car and the ambulance arrived at the scene with commendable speed. Ironically, one of the police officers was the PC Wright who had broken the news to Edmund Carton of his son's death. The other was Sergeant Donaldson.

They found a motorbike lying on its side under a stone wall, and the rider on the grass verge close by. A car was parked a few yards away. As they arrived, a man got out of the car and introduced himself.

'You may remember me, Sergeant Donaldson. I'm Basil Moore, the vicar at Little Chipping. I'd been visiting a very sick member of another church for which I'm responsible and was on my way home when I came upon this.'

'And it was you who phoned us, sir.'

'Yes. At once. From my car phone, as I said. I've taken off his crash helmet so that he can breathe more easily and I've covered him up with a rug to keep him warm. Otherwise, I've not touched anything.'

'Very sensible of you, sir,' said Donaldson. He was bending over the motorcyclist. 'Whew!' he added, recoiling.

'Yes,' said Moore. 'He has taken drink in a big way, poor man. The smell of gin is exceedingly strong, isn't it? He'll regret it in the morning.'

'He'll regret it in court when he recovers,' said Donaldson.

'It's Gavin Brail,' Wright said. 'I recognize him. He lives in Colombury and works at the Windrush Garage, Mr Field's place. He's made a fair mess of his bike.'

'But he seems OK, except possibly for a spot of concussion,' said the senior ambulance man. 'The luck of the drunk. He must have come along here at speed and simply ignored the corner and gone straight into the wall. I don't imagine that any other vehicle was concerned.'

'That reminds me,' Donaldson said. 'We heard from the station that someone else had reported the accident after you, Mr Moore, sir, but he didn't give his name. You must have seen his car, or whatever it was.'

The Reverend Basil Moore shook his head. 'No. I've seen no one. He wasn't behind me. He must have been ahead, but maybe he didn't have a car phone, and had to wait till he got to an ordinary phone to make the call. Is it important?'

'No, I shouldn't think so, sir.' Donaldson dismissed the second caller. 'Well, we'd better get Mr Gavin Brail to the hospital so he has no cause for complaint against the police. Thank you for your cooperation, sir. I don't expect we'll need to bother you about this matter again. It's obviously a perfectly straightforward accident, the result of drunk-driving.'

'You know where to find me, if necessary,' Moore said, getting into his car. He had had a tiring evening and wanted to be gone.

And it was left to PC Wright to wonder how Gavin Brail, whom he knew to be a pretty sober character, had got himself into this state, and why. But he didn't bother with the problem for long. He too was eager to get home – to his girlfriend.

6

Gavin Brail was in the habit of waking up each morning between six-fifteen and six-thirty. His ways were so set that he didn't need an alarm clock. As a rule he would go down to the kitchen, make himself and Rita cups of tea and bring them back to bed. Sometimes they would make love; the boys were not allowed to disturb them until seven.

Today was no exception in that Brail woke shortly before six-thirty. Otherwise, everything was different. He had begun to swing his legs out of bed before he realized that he was not at home, he was not wearing his pyjamas and there was no Rita beside him. But it didn't take him long to realize where he was. The curtained cubicle, the high narrow bed, the smell of disinfectant and the white gown he was dressed in, made his situation only too clear. He was in hospital somewhere.

It was a shock. How had he got there? Why was he here? There was nothing wrong with him, unless – What had those devils, whom Portman had set on him, done? He felt all right, but – He shivered and, suddenly cold, crawled back into bed. There was no sign of his clothes anywhere.

For several minutes he lay there, hugging himself and remembering the events of the previous evening. Portman – he assumed it was Portman – had delivered the money and he had collected it. Sadly Brail wondered what had happened to it. Then there had been that terrifying interlude in the van, when he had thought they were going to kill him and he had sworn to forget the red Toyota, Portman, Frankie Carton. He remembered clearly what was required of him.

After that there was a blank. He had no idea how he had

reached this hospital or what might have happened to bring him here, wherever here was. He wasn't sure that he wanted to know. He suspected that it was almost certainly something unpleasant, something to remind him of the dreadful threats they had made the night before. Nevertheless, he would have to face it. He couldn't stay cowering under the bedclothes for ever. Rita would be frantic if she had not been told where he was.

He found a bellpush by the bed and pressed it. Within minutes, a pretty young nurse appeared through the curtains. Another time he would have attempted to flirt with her, but today he wasn't in the mood.

'Good morning, Mr Brail,' she said. 'How are you feeling?'

'I'm fine.'

'Fine?' She sounded surprised. 'Not even a headache?'

'Why should I have a headache?'

She laughed. 'You ask me that after last night? So you'd like a nice breakfast?'

'I'd like my clothes, so that I can get out of here. And where is here? Colombury Hospital?'

'Yes, of course. And you can't leave, Mr Brail, not until the doctor's seen you. He may want you to stay on with us for a day or two.'

'Why?'

'In case you've got concussion. You don't remember, do you? I'm afraid you were very drunk last night, Mr Brail. When they brought you into casualty you reeked of gin.'

Gin? He never drank spirits. Too expensive. Someone – he could guess who – had poured gin over him. What else had they done? 'Gin doesn't give you concussion,' he ventured carefully.

'It does if you ride your motorbike into a stone wall. The police will have some questions for you later in the morning, I'm afraid.'

'I don't remember,' he said.

She laughed again. 'That's probably your best excuse. I'd stick to it if I were you. Incidentally, while I think to tell you, your wife's been informed and she'll be along as soon as your boys have gone to school.'

54

'Thank you.'

Brail was relieved that Rita wasn't still worrying about him, but she would expect an explanation. He would have to think of some plausible story for her – and for the police. Under his breath he cursed Portman.

'Now, there's a loo at the end of the ward,' the nurse said. 'You go along while I get your breakfast. What would you like, Mr Brail. You can have –'

'Just a pot of tea, please.'

Nevertheless, she brought him orange juice, toast and a boiled egg, and because it was there he ate it all, surprised by his own hunger until he realized that he had had nothing to eat since his midday meal the previous day. Then his visitors started to arrive.

The doctor was the first. He was about to go off night shift, but he was conscientious and gave Brail a thorough examination before agreeing there was nothing wrong with him, and he could be discharged after the police had been.

'You're a lucky man,' he said as he was going. 'You could easily have been killed. And you're lucky in another way. Obviously you couldn't be breathalysed as you were unconscious and through an oversight a sample of your blood was not taken for analysis, so I don't think the police can proceed very far.'

'I see,' said Brail weakly, and thought how right the doctor was; he could have been killed, easily, but not in the way the doctor imagined.

The next arrival was Rita, full of anxiety, but happy to see him sitting up in bed. She said she had phoned the Windrush Garage, and Mr Field had been very sympathetic. She didn't mention anything about Gavin having been drunk, raising his hopes that this aspect of the matter might not become general knowledge.

These hopes were reinforced by Sergeant Donaldson, who admitted that there was insufficient evidence to charge him with riding a motorcycle while under the influence of alcohol; nevertheless, he could be charged with dangerous driving and partially destroying a stone wall, the property of a Major Derwent.

'You've got a good character,' Donaldson said, 'and it's a first offence. Given any luck you'll get off with a caution and a fine and an order to pay for the repair of the wall. Now, what about this smell of gin? It's puzzling,' he added, echoing the doctor.

'I don't remember anything,' said Brail. 'All I know is that I didn't have a drink of any kind all day – and, what's more, I never touch spirits.'

'I see,' said Donaldson doubtfully. 'Well, all we can do is wait for the magistrate.'

In the event, the price was not unreasonable. Rita was more sympathetic than he had expected, his cronies treated him as something of a hero and, though, the fine and the damages came to more than two hundred pounds, to his amazement he discovered that the sum had been paid by an anonymous donor. His bike, however, was a write-off.

By a process of elimination, Brail decided that his benefactor must be Mr Field, his employer, though as Field didn't refer to it, Brail made no mention of it himself. Nevertheless, to show his appreciation, in the weeks that followed he worked hard and even volunteered for a couple of inconvenient jobs.

And gradually, after the traumatic experiences that had followed his attempt to blackmail Portman, he settled down to his normal way of life. He continued to hope that the police would discover the owner of the red Toyota that had killed Frankie Carton, and so would be led to Portman, but he knew it was wishful thinking, and he didn't intend to take any action. He had, he thought bitterly, learnt his lesson; he would never again tangle with the rich and powerful.

It was chance that made him change his mind, and take what he trusted would be only a minor risk.

On the first of December, Field called Brail into his office and gave him a month's notice. He said he was sorry, but business was not as brisk as it should be and for financial reasons he had to let one of his mechanics go. He had no complaint to make about Brail's work, and would give him an excellent reference. He also promised to allow Brail time off so that he might look for another job.

'You won't find anything in Colombury,' he said. 'But you might try Oxford – the Cowley Works – or Reading, where you were before.'

'I'll try Bristol first. I've relatives there,' Brail said sullenly.

He was stunned. He knew that Field was not telling the truth; the Windrush Garage was perfectly prosperous and there was more than enough work for the present technical staff. Why then was he being sacked? It couldn't be because of his motorbike accident, or Field wouldn't have paid his fine. No, it was something that had happened after that, some other filthy trick that Portman had played. Portman had told lies about him, or had bribed Field with the promise of business. Whatever it was, Portman was driving him and his family out of Colombury. But the bastard wasn't going to get away with it scot-free this time, Brail vowed to himself, though at the moment he had no idea what he might do to rectify the matter.

Christmas came and went. In the New Year, the Brails moved to Bristol. With the help of his brother-in-law, Gavin Brail found a job at much the same pay as he had received at the Windrush Garage, and the family settled down well. But his dismissal continued to rankle until he decided what to do.

During one lunch hour when he was alone at the garage, he went into the office and typed a letter to Edmund Carton, giving him what information he had concerning Frankie's death. He hoped Carton would at least go to the police and try to persuade them to reopen the case, which seemed to have completely dropped from the news; alternatively, there was always the possibility that he would take matters into his own hands.

Brail took the precaution of asking a fellow mechanic, who was going to London, to post the letter there, so he was confident that it wouldn't be traced to him. Then he settled down to wait. It was a poor, even amateurish, attempt at revenge, he told himself, but it was the best plan he could devise without putting himself at risk. If the letter brought no result he was no worse off, and there was a good chance that something might come of it.

The letter, marked *Personal*, arrived at Edmund Carton's small house outside Colombury on Saturday morning. Apart from bills and correspondence with editors and junk mail, he received almost no post, and he regarded the envelope with mild curiosity.

'Well, open it, Edmund, or you'll never know what's inside,' said Beth.

His sister had returned to Colombury with him after the holiday he had spent with her in Scotland. She was helping him clear up the house. She had persuaded him to rent it for a while, and come to live with her. Indeed, she hoped it would be a permanent arrangement, but Edmund refused to commit himself.

Edmund opened the letter and read it with surprise. He wondered why it had been sent to him and not to the police, and why the writer hadn't come forward before, when any-one with information concerning the accident had been requested to do so. There was something strange about the letter, he thought, apart from its anonymity. From the little knowledge he had of anonymous letters, which anyway he disliked on principle, they were either abusive or made accusations against individuals close to the addressee. But, though he knew of Sir Bertram Rocque and Christopher Portman, he had never met them and was indifferent to them. As to the letter, it was informative and surprisingly sympathetic in tone, not in the least abusive. Nevertheless, it was an unpleasant letter, disturbing, and he decided he wanted no part of it.

'What is it, Edmund? Why are you frowning so fiercely?' Beth demanded.

'Nothing important, Beth. A rather odd letter, that's all.'
'How odd?'

'About the car that killed Frankie. The writer claims to have identified it. I suspect he has a grudge against the sup-posed owner or he'd have gone to the police before now.'

Edmund got to his feet. 'I'm going upstairs to do some

more packing and clearing out. It's amazing how much stuff one collects.'

'May I see the letter?' Beth said, holding out her hand.

But Edmund had already tossed it into the fire. 'S-sorry,' he stammered.

He strode out of the living-room and took the stairs two at a time. He wished Beth wouldn't be so intrusive and possessive. Why should she expect to read his letters? He hoped that going to live with her wasn't a mistake, that she wouldn't encroach too endlessly on his privacy. She made him feel so stressed.

He went along to his workroom and sat at his desk, which was piled high with paper of various kinds, from magazine and newspaper cuttings to offprints of articles he had written himself. There were even a few chapters of a book he knew he would never finish now. It all needed to be sorted and packed in cartons, some to be shipped to Beth's house in Peebles, the rest to be left in the loft here – or thrown away. For a moment, he was tempted to take the whole lot into the garden and make a bonfire of it. It was the thought of Beth, who would certainly want an explanation for every armful that was added to the blaze, that dissuaded him.

Punctiliously he set to work, but he had achieved very little when Beth called up the stairs to tell him that it was after twelve. His thoughts had kept wandering – to Margaret, his long dead wife, to Frankie, who had been the product of their love, and to the anonymous letter he had just received. Although he had thrown the letter into the fire, he remembered the contents clearly. They worried him.

'Edmund! Have you forgotten that your friend is expected at twelve-thirty?'

This was Beth's second warning and Edmund, who had been lost in thought again, answered quickly, 'Coming, Beth! Coming!'

He washed his hands and ran a comb through his hair. Jocelyn Hauler was due for lunch. Since the dreadful evening that Frankie had been killed, he and Hauler, in spite of the disparity in their ages, had become friends. He hadn't seen Hauler since before Christmas, and was glad of the opportunity to say goodbye before he went to stay with Beth.

Jocelyn Hauler took the news badly. 'But you'll be coming back,' he said, a spoonful of soup halfway to his mouth. 'You're not going for good, are you, Edmund?'

It was Beth who answered. 'We'll have to see. Personally, I think Edmund would be well advised to sell this house and make a clean break. It has too many unhappy memories.'

'More happy ones,' Edmund said. 'I've arranged to let it for five months, Jocelyn. That will give me plenty of time to decide what I want to do. Luckily, my work isn't dependent on where I live.'

'Well then, this is goodbye,' Hauler said. 'Heaven knows where I'll be when you return – if you return – but it certainly won't be at Coriston. My contract was for three years, and I was told at the beginning of term that it wasn't to be renewed.'

'But why ever not?' Edmund was indignant. 'Frankie said you were a splendid teacher.'

Jocelyn Hauler shrugged. He couldn't explain, not even to Edmund; perhaps, because of Frankie, least of all to Edmund. The headmaster had been quite kind, but he had been blunt. He had said that he had no complaint about Hauler's teaching, and certainly no complaints about overt misconduct. Nevertheless, Hauler's personal relations with some of the younger boys appeared to some of the masters and prefects as not altogether desirable. When his contract expired, it would probably be a sensible idea if he were to choose a career other than schoolmastering.

'We'll keep in touch, I hope, Edmund,' Jocelyn said.

'Of course. Of course.'

Edmund half-expected an explanation later when Beth was washing up and the two men were alone, but when none came he was too tactful to ask. Instead, he told Jocelyn Hauler about the anonymous letter he had received, and they discussed it until Beth rejoined them and Hauler said he must go.

On that same Saturday, Christopher Portman and Simon Wayne were having a late lunch together. Portman had flown in from New York earlier that morning and they had had a great deal of news to exchange. They continued to discuss business matters over the meal, and it wasn't until they reached the cheese stage that Wayne turned to more personal subjects.

'Incidentally, Chris,' he said, 'you may be interested to hear that Mr Brail and family have gone to live in Bristol.'

'How do you know that?'

'Field told me. I bought some petrol from the Windrush Garage, and noticed that Brail wasn't around and saw they had a new man. I asked Field what had happened to Brail – it was quite a natural inquiry on my part. Field told me that Brail was a good mechanic, but somehow he had never trusted the man, and finally he decided to get rid of him.'

'Do you think his sacking was connected with that accident we manufactured?'

'I'd guess it had some influence, but it wasn't the decisive factor. Anyway, I gather the bastard's got a job in Bristol and they've settled down there. For heaven's sake, Chris, you've nothing to reproach yourself about. Brail deserved all he got and more. You were damned generous to pay his fine.'

'I didn't do it for him. I've no pity for blackmailers, but I couldn't let his wife and kids suffer, which is what would have happened, I guess. Luckily, his bike was insured.'

'OK.'

Wayne wasn't prepared to argue. He just hoped for Chris Portman's sake that the departure of Gavin Brail and his family from the district would bring about the end of the whole miserable affair.

PART II

7

'Good morning!'

Andrea Rocque breezed into the sitting-room at Wych-wood Manor. She was a tall, slender woman in her mid-thirties, but she looked younger. Always beautiful, with a perfect oval face and large violet-coloured eyes, she was particularly radiant this July morning. She was happy.

'Good morning, darling.' Bertram's tired expression bright-ened at the sight of his wife.

''Morning.' Daphne Mariner regarded her sister-in-law with interest. 'You're very early this morning, Andrea, and looking very smart. Are you going somewhere?'

Andrea sat down at the small round table at the end of the sitting-room, where they had all their meals unless there were guests, which these days was an infrequent occurrence. She smoothed the skirt of her silk suit over her knees, glanced with distaste at the bacon and eggs the others were eating, and helped herself to coffee and toast.

'I'm catching the eight-ten to London,' she said.

'London? Why on earth are you going to London?' This from Bertram. London was a place he avoided, unless a visit were essential for some reason.

'Primarily to buy myself a dress for Chris Portman's party next month.'

'I thought that was what you were doing in Oxford yes-terday.'

'I couldn't find anything I liked.'

This was a lie. She hadn't bothered to look. She had spent most of the day at a beauty parlour, having a facial, her blonde hair tinted, her nails manicured, her body massaged

– the full treatment. It had made her feel so wonderful that she had wished she could have gone straight to Chris Portman's bed, but that had to wait until today.

'Do you *need* a new dress?' Daphne asked.

'Yes!' Andrea buttered her toast carefully. 'After all, Chris doesn't often give a party, does he? Oh, I know he entertains quite a lot, but that's mostly for his business friends and acquaintances from London and abroad. This is different – a party for his real friends and neighbours to celebrate the tenth anniversary of his purchase of Charlbury Hall. It's a lovely idea.'

'I don't see that in the present state of our family finances it warrants an expensive new dress,' Daphne said.

'You might not, but I do,' Andrea retorted. 'Anyway, who said anything about it being an expensive dress?'

'When did you last buy a dress that wasn't expensive?' Daphne asked bitterly.

Andrea didn't bother to answer. She smiled at the thought of how annoyed Daphne would be if she knew how much the beauty salon in Oxford had charged her. She herself had been a little shocked by the size of the bill. But she didn't regret it. She needed to look her best today.

Chris was taking her to lunch at the Connaught, and afterwards they would go back to his flat, and make love. Thank goodness he seemed to have got over the difficult mood he was in for so long after that wretched Carton boy had been killed. It hadn't been her fault. It had been an accident, and it wouldn't have done any good if she had stopped. But Chris had taken it hard. Indeed, it was only quite recently, after all these months, that she had begun to feel sure of him again.

Andrea finished her coffee and stood up. 'Well, I'm off. See you tonight. Goodbye, darlings. It's all right if I take the Toyota and leave it at the station?'

'Of course. We shan't be needing it,' said Bertram. 'Goodbye. Enjoy yourself, darling,' he added as his wife bent and planted a kiss on his forehead. 'Though why she wants to go to London on a lovely summer's day like this beats me,' he remarked to Daphne, as the door closed behind Andrea.

'I think she may find life here rather dull,' Daphne said; she was always careful never to criticize Andrea to Bertram.

Bertram sighed. 'Yes, and it is, except to people used to it. We'll have to try to do something about it, but with money being so damned short it isn't easy. At least she's enjoying her riding lessons.'

Which you can ill afford, Daphne thought, but she didn't comment aloud. She was fond of her brother and, if he spoiled Andrea and chose to turn a blind eye to her infidelities and extravagances, she was prepared to accept the situation, though on occasion it annoyed her. This morning had been one of those occasions. Andrea had bought a new dress just before Christmas, to add to a fairly extensive wardrobe, and she had no need of yet another for Chris Portman's party. She wondered what Bertram would have said if she had suggested buying a new dress to replace her blue that everyone knew so well. She could imagine. He would have called it a quite unnecessary expense.

Bertram, in what he considered a spirit of fairness, had decreed that the three of them – Andrea, Daphne and himself – should be entitled to equal personal allowances from the estate. What he hadn't taken into account was Andrea's reaction. While he and Daphne worked extremely hard to make the market garden profitable and poured most of their 'allowances' back into the business of keeping up the Manor, Andrea spent every penny on herself and contributed nothing. Once, challenged by Daphne, she had pointed out that she was Bertram's wife, not his dependent sister.

It was a remark that Daphne had never been able to forget or forgive. But she was a practical woman, and knew that, for Bertram's sake as well as her own, she had to accept the position. Besides, though she would have loathed to admit it, she realized that if she was honest with herself, what really riled her was the affair she was sure Andrea was having with Christopher Portman. She herself had loved Chris Portman ever since they had been children together, and she had been the small girl who had tagged along after the two boys. But the gardener's son had gone away, and she had married Stewart Mariner. Now, years later, she found that her feelings hadn't changed, but to Chris she was still Bertram's young sister, and he preferred Bertram's wife.

'Daphne!'

'Yes? Sorry, Bertram, what did you say?'

'What's the matter with you, Daphne? Are you going deaf? I said that the first thing I propose to do this morning is inspect the heating system in the greenhouses. If it won't last another winter, this is the time to renew it, not when we're deep in snow.'

'We can't afford it, Bertram. We're horribly overdrawn as it is.'

'We can't not afford it. I'll have a word with Carmichael.' Bertram turned and stomped out of the room, followed by Judy, his old retriever.

Daphne shook her head. She doubted if the present bank manager, who was young and new, would be as obliging as his predecessor, and even he had refused to grant them the last increase they had requested. But it was useless arguing with Bertram. As she started to collect the dirty breakfast dishes on to a tray, in order to take them out to the kitchen, she wondered how much longer they could go on amassing debts which they had no hope of ever repaying. It was a bleak outlook. And she thought with added bitterness of Andrea jaunting off to London.

'Daphne! Daphne! Where the hell are you?' Bertram stormed into the house.

Daphne came out of the kitchen. 'I'm here. What on earth's the trouble?'

'The trouble?' Bertram was practically inarticulate with anger. 'Come and look! See what your carelessness has done! You talk about not wasting money, and then you – you –'

Bertram had become increasingly irritable lately. He also was worried about their finances, the possibility that the market garden might go bankrupt and, Daphne suspected, about Andrea's growing lack of cooperation. But she couldn't remember seeing him in such a rage for a very long time, in fact, not since she had destroyed his signed Beatles poster thirty-odd years ago, when they had both been children.

Daphne meekly followed Bertram into the garden and around the back of the stables to the henhouse. Here she stopped, her mouth slightly open, while Bertram pointed with a trembling finger.

'Oh no!' she cried. 'Oh no!'

It was a sickening sight. The cockerel and at least half a dozen hens were dead, their heads and wings torn off, their bodies savaged, feathers everywhere. Punch, Judy's young son, ran forward to sniff at the cockerel's body, and Bertram called him to heel. He came reluctantly and, remembering his training, laid the remains of a bird at Bertram's feet.

'Good dog!' Bertram said automatically, and bent to give him a pat.

'The poor things,' Daphne said. 'They must have been terrified. How on earth did it happen?'

'You ask me?' Bertram was curt. 'Obviously you didn't shut the door properly and a fox got in, or a feral cat.'

'I did shut the door properly. I'm always very careful.'

'You weren't very careful yesterday. Daphne, the hens are your responsibility. You feed them. You look after them. No one else would have gone in there, and no animal could open the door for itself.'

'I know that, but –'

'And that's not all. The hens that escaped from the beast's attack are out rooting about among those young plants I put in yesterday. They've already ruined half of them.'

'I'm sorry, Bertram, but truly I did –'

'I suggest you round up the loose hens before they do any more damage, Daphne, and then clear up this mess. I'm going along to the greenhouses.'

Bertram strode off, accompanied by the two dogs, and Daphne stood, fighting back her anger. She *had* shut the door of the henhouse. She was absolutely sure. As she'd told Bertram, she was always very careful. And anyway, he had no right to speak to her like that, as if she were just an inefficient employee.

Daphne squared her shoulders. It would be a filthy business cleaning up, and Bertram had made it plain she would get no help. To hell with him, she thought. Nevertheless, she knew she had better start by rounding up the remaining hens.

Andrea arrived home shortly before seven in a taxi. She was laden with parcels, and on the edge of being a little tight. She dumped her packages on the sofa in the sitting-room and collapsed beside them.

'I'm absolutely exhausted,' she said.

Bertram looked up from his newspaper. 'I'm not surprised. You seem to have bought half London.'

'Darling Bertram, you don't really mind, do you? You said I might have a dress, and I got an absolute bargain at a little boutique off Knightsbridge, but I had to get one or two accessories to go with it.'

'Well, I hope you enjoyed your day.'

'Yes. It was great fun.' Andrea hesitated. It had been bad luck that she and Chris had found themselves lunching at a table next to Philip Midvale, the chief constable of the Thames Valley Police Force, and his wife, both friends of Bertram's. It was unlikely that Midvale would mention the encounter to Bertram, but his wife might. 'And you'll never guess. I bumped into Chris Portman in Harrods, and he took me to lunch at the Connaught.'

'What a coincidence!' Daphne said before she could stop herself.

'Yes, wasn't it?' Andrea smiled at her sweetly. 'And it wasn't the only one. Philip Midvale and his wife were lunching there too, at the next table.'

So that's why you told us, thought Daphne, who had no belief in Andrea's coincidental meeting with Portman. Andrea and Chris had been enjoying a day together in London as planned, while she – she – Her eyes began to fill with tears, and abruptly she stood up, angry with herself that she minded so much.

'I'll go and see if Alice needs any help with the supper,' she said. Alice, the elderly housekeeper, with a part-time woman from the village, now represented the entire indoor staff of Wychwood Manor. 'We should be eating in about forty minutes.'

As she left the sitting-room, Andrea said, 'Bertram, I had to take a taxi from the station. The Toyota wouldn't start. I even asked one of the porters to try, but he couldn't start it either.'

'Damn!' Bertram said. Apart from the cost of a taxi from Colombury station, it meant that the car would have to be collected and probably repaired, or at least serviced. More money. 'Well, it's much too late to do anything about it now. I'll see to it in the morning.'

'Right.' Andrea began to gather her parcels before going upstairs. 'I must go and change. I've been in this suit all day.' That, too, was a lie.

Bertram nodded and returned to his newspaper. He didn't catch the exasperated glance that Andrea directed at him. Her day had not been as wonderful as she had anticipated. The shopping had been very successful, the luncheon — except for the worrying presence of the Midvales — most enjoyable, but there had been something lacking in Christopher's love-making. Immediately afterwards, pleading a business engagement, he had put her into a taxi and sent her off to Paddington earlier than she expected. She had sat and shivered, the weather having suddenly changed, and the temperature dropped ten degrees.

Cold and miserable, she had finally gone into the station bar, and ordered a brandy which had cheered her up, and before it was time for her train she had had another. These, added to the amount of champagne she had drunk during the day, had caused her to be slightly drunk, and she hadn't dared risk driving back to the Manor from the station at Colombury. Since Frankie Carton's death, she had been exceedingly circumspect. She had made straight for the taxi rank and not bothered to check on the Toyota.

Bertram, she thought as she unpacked and hung up the new dress, would be pleased when he found nothing wrong with the car the next morning. He wouldn't be so pleased when he discovered how much the dress had cost; it was certainly not true that it had been a bargain. But once she had tried it on, there had been no question but that she must have it. After all, she deserved some pretty things.

She had been attracted by Bertram's title, his ancient name and a house that had been in the family for more than a century. What she hadn't realized, before she married him, was how poor his prospects were, and how titles and names and a house were no compensations for a chronic lack of money – a lack which seemed to be steadily growing worse. And not for the first time she wished she could be Christopher Portman's wife.

8

The next morning, Daphne was in the office, a small and cluttered room at one end of Wychwood Manor. It was a Friday, the day on which the woman from the village and the garden hands were paid; Alice, the housekeeper, received a monthly salary. The paperwork involved in running the house and the market garden was considerable and time-consuming, as Daphne had discovered since David Garson, who had been Bertram's assistant, had been sacked, and she had taken on the job. Coping with the interminable cash-flow problem was a special nightmare and a near impossibility.

She was frowning over a column of figures, which added up to a different total each time she tried, and was wondering why on earth they didn't buy a cheap calculator, when Bertram came in. It was early for his mid-morning break, and she looked up in surprise.

'Something wrong?'

'Some yobbo has thrown a couple of bricks through one of the greenhouses. Two panes smashed and another two cracked. Glass all over the place and, of course, it rained last night so there's a pretty mess.'

'That's too bad!' exclaimed Daphne. 'Why should anyone want to do that?'

'God knows! Sheer vandalism, I suppose.'

Daphne got up to put on the electric kettle for coffee and the telephone trilled. 'It hasn't stopped ringing all the morning,' Daphne said. 'I've several orders for raspberries.'

'Won't be ready till next week,' Bertram replied. 'If that's Field, let me speak to him.'

'Hello!' Daphne said, and shook her head at her brother. 'It's Simon Wayne,' she mouthed, and listened intently. 'That's very good of you, Simon. Are you sure it isn't too much of a nuisance? We could fetch them —' There was a pause while she listened again before saying, 'No, we can't think how it happened. We seem to be jinxed at the moment. Everything's going wrong. OK then. We're most grateful. Come at the right time for a drink.'

'What is it now?' Bertram asked quickly as Daphne replaced the receiver.

'The horses,' Daphne said. 'The gate was left open and two of them wandered out of the field and into the lanes. They could have been killed or caused a bad accident. Fortunately, one of the staff from the Hall spotted them, and they've been rounded up. Old Mollie, incidentally, had enough sense to stay put.'

'Are they sound?'

'Apparently. We've been lucky. Belle's slightly lame because of a small cut on her left hind. Nothing serious. Simon said if it was OK with us, he'd bring them back later this morning.'

'That's very good of him.' Bertram heaved a sigh. 'As you say, we're lucky the damage is no worse. You know, Daphne, that gate didn't open itself. What do you bet that whoever chucked those bricks through the greenhouse also let the horses out?'

And opened the henhouse door, Daphne thought. She made the coffee and handed her brother a cup. 'Are you expecting a call from Field?'

'Yes. I phoned him earlier and asked him if he'd send a mechanic along to the station to see if he can start the Toyota. I don't believe there can be much wrong with it, and I'm hoping either you or I might take the bus in later today and collect it. The van will be busy with deliveries all the afternoon.'

'Couldn't Andrea go?'

'She's not too well. I think she overdid it yesterday.'

'Really?' It was a poor and, for Daphne, an uncharacteristic attempt to sound sarcastic, and she tried to cover it by adding

74

quickly, 'The car's locked, I'm sure. How will Field get into it without a key?'

'I thought of that. He says he's got a variety of car keys at the garage, and it should be no problem.'

'Right. I'll let you know when he calls, and, Bertram, you're looking tired. I'll fetch the Toyota.'

Bertram grinned at her. 'Thanks a lot, Daphne. I don't know what I'd do without you. Sorry I've been so irritable lately but, as you're only too well aware, the going isn't particularly easy at the moment.'

Bertram finished his coffee and strode out of the room. Daphne returned to the accounts. She couldn't agree with Bertram's implication that they were merely going through a bad patch; that suggested they would eventually emerge from it, and she saw no possibility of this happening. On the contrary, with their debts mounting steadily, she wondered yet once more how much longer they could continue as they were.

Field telephoned shortly before lunch. Bertram and Daphne were giving Simon Wayne the promised drink for returning the two wandering horses; Andrea, who was indeed feeling rather unwell, had decided to spend the day in bed.

Bertram was some time on the phone and Daphne, who had been explaining their growing list of minor calamities and how the Toyota happened to be in the station parking lot in Colombury, said, 'I can't think what's keeping him. I hope there's nothing seriously wrong with the car —'

She stopped as Bertram came striding back into the room, his face set in grim lines. He flung himself into a chair and shook his head slowly as if he had received a shock. For a moment he didn't speak, and Daphne and Wayne stared at him in surprise.

Then he said, 'You'll not believe what Field has just told me.' He didn't wait for them to ask any questions, but continued, 'He sent a mechanic to the station to have a look at the Toyota, as I asked him, and he found it — he found it had been vandalized!'

'Vandalized?' Daphne was appalled. 'In Colombury station car park? Oh, Bertram, no.'

'How badly?' Wayne asked.

'One of the outside rear-view mirrors was broken off and the radio aerial snapped. But that's not the worst of it. The paintwork has been badly scored with a sharp instrument, either a knife or a pair of scissors or a tool of some kind. When the mechanic reported this to Field, he went along himself, and he says we really need a new door and side panel, which will be an expensive job. Oddly enough, the damage seems to be all on one side – the near side. And another odd thing is that, according to Field, the engine started immediately, and the car's going like a bird.'

'What about the interior, Bertram?'

'Fine, Simon. The vandal never tried to get into the car. It looks as if the damage was probably the work of a couple of minutes, someone passing by who thought he'd have a bit of fun, or possibly didn't think and just acted automatically.'

'But we have to pay for it.' Daphne was bitter.

'I'm afraid so. Field complained to the station master, who said people leave their cars in the park at their own risk. And the police took particulars, but they're not seriously interested and hold out no hope of finding the culprit.'

'It's a damned shame,' Wayne said. 'Won't your insurance cover it?'

'I don't think so. We've only got third party and fire and theft, not comprehensive. Anyway, I asked Field to replace the mirror and the aerial which aren't big jobs, but to leave the door and the side panel. With any luck my garage in Little Chipping will be able to touch up the scratch marks and save the bulk of the expense.'

Wayne nodded, though he didn't think much of the idea. 'It will depend how deep the scoring is,' he said.

Daphne didn't find the remark encouraging. She thought of the dead cockerel and his hens – she was positive she had secured the henhouse – the bricks through the greenhouse, the horses let loose, and now the Toyota. She couldn't believe they were all coincidental. But the alternative, that someone was deliberately trying to cause them distress and anxiety was frightening. Who would want to do that? They had no enemies. And yet it couldn't be casual malice.

76

'Anyway, if you need any more help, you've only to ask,' Wayne said.

'Yes, I know. Thanks,' Bertram said. 'But I hope this will be the end of our disasters.' He spoke lightly, but Daphne could see he was very upset.

Four days later, Alice, the housekeeper, came into the room where the family were having breakfast. She apologized for interrupting them.

'I'm sorry to bother you, Sir Bertram, but do you know where the dogs are?'

'No. I thought they were with you, Alice.'

'I let them out first thing as usual, sir, but they've not come back in, to my knowledge.'

'They must be somewhere around in the garden,' Bertram said carelessly, his mind on other worries.

He saw no reason to be anxious. Admittedly, Judy, the older dog, mostly joined them for breakfast in the hope of titbits, but Punch was erratic. He liked to go rabbiting, though he never caught one, and would disappear for hours.

It was not until lunch that the question of the dogs' whereabouts again arose. The morning had been busy. Daphne had been helping Bertram pick raspberries and Andrea, who wasn't particularly interested in the dogs anyhow, had agreed to walk across the fields to Little Chipping, where the local garage had done its best with the damage to the Toyota, to collect the car.

Andrea returned just before lunch and the three of them were inspecting the Toyota, the value of which had obviously deteriorated since it had suffered at the hands of the vandals, and were about to return to the house when Daphne said suddenly, 'Where *are* the dogs, Bertram? Have you seen them today?'

'No. Frankly, we've been so busy I haven't given them a thought. One gets so used to having them about that I hadn't noticed they weren't there. But surely –'

No one had seen them. They hadn't come into the kitchen for their early morning biscuits. Now anxiety grew. Where on earth were the dogs, Judy and her son, Punch?

'They must be somewhere in the grounds,' Bertram said. 'They're not like the horses. They wouldn't stray and they certainly wouldn't allow themselves to be kidnapped. You two go on into lunch and I'll look for them.'

'I'll help you,' Daphne said at once. 'Lunch doesn't matter. It's cold today and it can wait.'

In the event it was Bertram who found the animals. They were near a stone wall that bounded part of the property, and beyond which was a public path. They were lying on the ground within a yard of each other. There was a white rim around their muzzles and flies had settled on them. They had been dead for some time.

Bertram stared at them in disbelief. Who could have done this, deliberately poisoned two beautiful dogs, and why? Tears blinded him. He had loved Judy and Punch. Then anger took over from grief, and he swore aloud.

Bertram Rocque was in many ways a simple man. His ambitions had never been those of a high-flyer. He had expected to inherit from his already elderly father – he had been born late, as an only child – and to live the life of a country gentleman, hunting, shooting, caring for the estate and his tenants, marrying and raising a family. Of course, he was an anachronism as, he soon discovered, his father had also been.

Sir David Rocque, Bart., left few debts, but even less money. His much younger widow was killed in a hunting accident soon after her husband's death, and the death duties imposed on the estate were heavy. Daphne, after a failed marriage, was living at home, and Bertram had recently married the glamorous Andrea. It was not an auspicious moment and, as a result, after almost everything had been sold that could be sold, the market garden was born. But neither Eton nor Oxford had imbued Bertram with a good business sense and, in spite of Daphne's efforts, it hadn't flourished.

Now, Bertram thought bitterly, not only were they in desperate financial straits, but they seemed to have acquired a personal enemy. The bricks through the greenhouse and the loose horses might have been the work of a casual vandal, even the damage to the Toyota – but not the poisoning of Judy and Punch.

'And don't forget the henhouse,' Daphne said when he told her about the dogs, adding their deaths to the growing list of bizarre events. 'I did shut the door properly, you know.'

'Yes. I believe you. I'm sorry.'

'Bertram, this can't go on. We must call the police.'

'I'm calling Peter White first.' White was the local vet. 'He'll want to do a postmortem. It may help the police, though I don't have much hope.'

'Well, something's got to be done, or God knows what will happen next,' said Daphne desperately.

It was a miserable lunch. None of them felt like eating, and what passed for casual conversation was stilted. There was really only one topic worth discussing, but by common consent they avoided it. It was a relief when the meal was over. After lunch, Andrea disappeared to her room; both Bertram and Daphne had noticed that she had seemed unexpectedly upset about the dogs. Daphne went to superintend the garden hands, and Bertram to wait for the vet.

Peter White arrived at two o'clock. He was a cheerful young man, and popular in the district for he never refused to come out to a sick animal, whatever the time and whatever the weather. He was as angry as Bertram when he saw the bodies.

'Wicked!' he said. 'Wicked! I'd have no mercy on whoever was responsible for this.'

'It can't have been accidental?' Bertram was tentative.

'No way. The white on their muzzles is quite distinctive. I'll have to do a PM, of course, but it's my guess someone bought two juicy steaks and soaked them thoroughly in rat poison – someone who has a grudge against you. He wasn't walking around carrying poisoned meat on the off chance that he found a suitable wall to throw it over, was he? Not unless he's a mental case.'

'It's not a pleasant thought.'

'I'm sure it isn't. Have you had any other troubles, Bertram? There have been rumours –'

'There have been two or three unusual incidents,' Bertram admitted reluctantly.

'OK.' Peter White was quick. 'I'll mind my own business, but I would advise you to go to the police.'

'I have phoned them. I hope you'll answer any questions they may have.'

'Certainly. I should be delighted to do my bit towards catching whoever committed this crime, but it'll take a couple of days for me to make a formal report. Meanwhile, if I bring up my van as close as possible, perhaps one of your men would help me get the poor dogs inside.'

'I'll help you myself,' Bertram said.

It didn't take long. First Punch, then Judy, were lifted on to a stretcher and carried to the van. Peter White promised to be in touch as soon as possible, said goodbye, and drove off, leaving an unhappy and depressed Bertram Rocque.

'You seem to have been in the wars recently, Sir Bertram.' Sergeant Donaldson smiled thinly.

'Yes, it would seem so.' Bertram did his best to sound indifferent; he disliked to think of his private affairs becoming part of local gossip, as it would appear, from what Peter White and Donaldson had said, they were. 'What can you do about it, Sergeant?'

'First of all, sir, give me the details of the earlier incidents, if we may call them that. WPC Digby here will make notes.'

Bertram hesitated, but could see no alternative. After all, he had called in the police and he must cooperate. He outlined the situation at Wychwood Manor, and added, 'So what can you do to help me, Sergeant?'

'Not very much about the earlier incidents, I'm afraid. You should have called us in when they occurred, if I may say so, sir. However, we may get a lead on the poisoning of your dogs if the stuff was bought locally. We'll make inquiries.'

'Thank you.' Bertram was brusque.

'Now, before you show us the scene of the crime, as it

were, perhaps you wouldn't mind answering a few questions, sir.'

'I've already given you all the information I can.'

'You told us you have no idea who might be making these attacks on you and your household, sir, but there are surely too many of them to be coincidences.'

It was more or less what Peter White had said, and Bertram knew it to be true. 'Sergeant, if you're saying I've got an enemy you may be right, but I've no idea who it might be.'

'What about your staff, sir? Have you got rid of any of them recently?'

Bertram hesitated. 'I let my assistant, David Garson, go for – for financial reasons. I haven't replaced him.'

'Do you have an address for him, sir?' WPC Digby looked up from her notebook.

'No, I'm afraid not.'

'So you've not kept in touch?' Donaldson was triumphant.

'No. Nevertheless, Sergeant, I'm positive these – these incidents were nothing to do with Garson. He would never have harmed the dogs. He was devoted to them.'

'If you say so, sir. Neighbours, then? Some of these farmers can get pretty stroppy if they're crossed in any way.'

Bertram shook his head. He was tired of the interrogation, which he was sure was a waste of time, and he had no faith in Sergeant Donaldson. He wondered if he should go over Donaldson's head and appeal to Philip Midvale, but, though he would have called the chief constable a friend, he decided at once that an approach to him would be an unwarranted imposition. Nevertheless, they needed help, or at least advice, and he thought of Christopher Portman.

9

'Who was that on the phone?'

Bertram, a towel wrapped around his waist, came out of the bathroom, which separated the dressing-room where he normally slept from the main bedroom. Andrea had already bathed and was sitting at her dressing-table. They were preparing to go to Christopher Portman's party.

'No one,' she said dismissively. 'A wrong number.' Her back was to him but he could see her face reflected in the mirror, a fact she hadn't realized.

'Are you all right?' As soon as he had spoken Bertram knew it was a question that would annoy Andrea, but her facial expression was so strange that he didn't think what he was saying. 'Darling, you're looking unwell. Are you sure you're all right?' He knew he was making the situation worse by persisting, but he was worried.

'Of course I'm all right. Why shouldn't I be?'

'I don't know. That phone call –'

'I told you. It was a wrong number.'

'If it was, then – fine.'

But Bertram knew that Andrea had lied. She had always had a propensity for adjusting the truth to suit herself, and there was no point in arguing with her. Obvious distrust only made her more obstinate. Nevertheless, he couldn't help continuing to wonder about the telephone call. He was not a fool . . . He was well aware that she wasn't the most faithful of wives and he guessed, though he had no definite proof, that she and Chris Portman had been lovers, and probably still were. However, a phone call from him wouldn't have upset her to such an extent. She had looked – he searched for the word, and came up with 'frightened'.

'Perhaps you'd do up my zip,' Andrea said, stepping into her dress, which was a sparkling violet sheath, the colour of her eyes.

'With pleasure.' Bertram, considering it his privilege, planted a row of light kisses down her spine before he drew up the zip. 'There's no doubt you'll be the most beautiful woman at the party,' he said.

Andrea turned and kissed him on the lips. 'Good! I hope that will please you.'

'It always does,' he said.

Their tiff, if it could be called a tiff, was over.

It was with some distaste that Daphne regarded herself in the long mirror in her bedroom. She was heartily tired of the blue evening dress she was wearing, and she imagined that everyone else at the party would be equally bored with it. She had had it for years. She couldn't remember how many. There was even a small tear in the skirt, where she had caught her heel in it the Christmas before last, and which she had never bothered to repair.

Collecting her purse and a mink jacket that had belonged to her mother, she went downstairs to find Alice. The old housekeeper was in the kitchen, preparing her evening meal.

'You're looking very pretty tonight, Miss Daphne,' Alice said.

Daphne laughed, and ignored the compliment. 'Alice, listen. You know we're going to Charlbury Hall, so that's where you can find us. If anything untoward should happen you must telephone at once. You mustn't hesitate.'

'And spoil your evening, Miss Daphne?' Alice shook her head. 'It's not as if you went to many parties.'

'That doesn't matter.'

'Miss Daphne, don't worry.'

'I can't help it. I don't like leaving you alone for such a long time. I've no idea when we'll be back, but almost certainly not till one or two in the morning. Normally, I wouldn't mind, but there have been such a lot of strange happenings at the Manor recently, as you know, and – '

'As everyone else in the neighbourhood knows, after that article in the *Courier*.' Alice sniffed. 'Horrid publicity for us all. Life isn't what it used to be when your dear father and mother were alive, Miss Daphne.'

While she agreed, Daphne was not encouraged by Alice's remark. It was years since her parents had died, but the old housekeeper spoke of the events as if they were last week and, though Alice still worked hard – harder than she should at her age – she was apt to live in the past. The chances that she would cope efficiently if there were an emergency were slight.

But there was nothing more Daphne could do, except to repeat her admonition to telephone the Hall if any problem arose and, having said goodbye to Alice, she joined Bertram and Andrea. She wasn't particularly looking forward to the party, but she knew she would have hated to miss it.

'Sir Bertram and Lady Rocque – and Mrs Mariner!'

Christopher Portman was receiving his guests at the entrance to the large drawing-room, which for the occasion had been turned into a ballroom. It wasn't often that he entertained what he laughingly called 'the County' but, when he did, he liked to do it in style. Daphne had tried to hold back, but still found herself announced by the butler, as if, she thought cynically, she were Andrea's lady-in-waiting.

Christopher kissed Andrea on the cheek and she pirouetted in front of him. It was her way of claiming that they were at least old and dear friends, and he was a man with whom she could be familiar.

'I hope you like my new dress, Chris.'

'Beautiful, and made more so by its wearer.'

Andrea laughed and Bertram, who liked Andrea to be admired, grinned as he shook hands with his host; he reminded himself that he must make an opportunity to ask Christopher's advice about the wretched persecution they were suffering. But now was not the moment. Christopher had turned to Daphne and kissed her.

'I won't ask if you like my dress, Chris. It's scarcely new to you,' she said lightly.

'No, perhaps not. But it suits you. Some things wear well – like people. Others don't.'

'Lord and Lady Mortland!'

Automatically, Daphne moved on as the Mortlands came forward to be welcomed by their host. She could feel her heart hammering and told herself she was being absurd, putting too much meaning into a few casual words. Of course Chris was fond of her. He had known her a very long time, since they were children, and they were friends – but not more than friends.

'And just what was Christopher whispering to you about?' Andrea demanded.

'Just making a joke about my old dress,' Daphne replied, taking a glass of champagne from a tray held out to her by a waiter.

Simon Wayne came up to greet them and asked Daphne to dance. Other friends joined the Rocques. More guests were arriving. Champagne was circulating. It would clearly be a good party and it was soon well under way.

Andrea, as always, was a centre of attraction, with no shortage of partners, and Christopher had his duty as a host to consider, so it was some while before he was able to claim her. Normally, Andrea wouldn't have minded, but tonight she was eager to speak to him, and the dance floor with the energetic playing of the band offered comparative privacy.

'Oh, Chris, at last! I need to talk to you, Chris, darling. I've had two quite spooky telephone calls. One on the Friday the dogs were found dead, poisoned. You know about that, don't you, and all our other troubles?'

'What I've learnt from Simon and that rather lurid piece in the *Courier*. I've been extremely busy this week.'

'I know. I tried to get in touch a number of times after the first call, but you were either away or in conference. Then nothing more happened and I thought – But tonight, while I was dressing to come here and Bertram was in the bathroom – Oh, Chris!'

For a moment, Andrea clung close to him, but Christopher

Portman, conscious of an amused grin from a nearby guest who happened to be dancing with Daphne, held her away from him. 'Anonymous calls, I assume. Male?'

'Yes, I think so. The voice was quite deep, obviously disguised.'

'What did he say?'

'It was much the same both times. I don't remember the exact words, but it was something like, "This is a warning, Lady Rocque. There is worse to come. You must pay for your sins". It wasn't funny, Chris. It was frightening. I felt threatened.'

'Did you give your name when you answered the phone?'

'Yes. I usually do.'

'But it was chance you answered, so there was nothing personal about it, Andrea. Have you told Bertram?'

'No. Chris, I – I wondered if the calls and the other – er – incidents, as we seem to call them, could conceivably be connected with that dreadful accident we had last year.'

Christopher raised his eyebrows. It hadn't escaped his notice that Andrea had apportioned him at least equal blame for Frankie Carton's death, and this annoyed him. He was sure that whatever she pretended, she was perfectly well aware of the facts. But he considered what she had said.

'I should think it most unlikely. That accident was months ago. If there was a connection, why the long delay? Then the attacks have been directed far more at Bertram and Daphne than at you and –' Christopher gave a sardonic grin '– and not at all at me.'

'Well, if these so-called incidents continue, I shall go away for a while, have a holiday. I suppose you wouldn't think of joining me, Chris?'

'No, Andrea. I'm much too busy at present. But thank you for the invitation.'

Christopher had spoken lightly, as if the invitation had not been serious, but both of them knew that it had been and that the refusal was definite. Fortunately, at that point the dance ended and the band started to play a hot South American number. Some of the older guests retreated. Simon

Wayne, in an immediate response to a meaningful glance from Christopher, claimed Andrea.

Not long afterwards, the band leader announced an interval for supper, and everyone moved slowly into the dining-room where an elaborate buffet was waiting for them.

Watching them go, Christopher Portman, in a rare moment of self-doubt, asked himself if this kind of life was what he really wanted. When he had first bought Charlbury Hall he had seen it as the home he had always yearned for, and mentally had peopled it with a wife and children and friends. He still loved the house, but he used it too much as an office centre and a place to entertain business colleagues or clients. He had neither wife nor children and, apart from Simon Wayne and the inhabitants of Wychwood Manor, almost no close friends. Even the Manor crowd were becoming a problem; Bertram Rocque, whom once he would have counted among his friends, now, because of his affair with Andrea, made him feel embarrassed and a little ashamed. He supposed there was still time – he wasn't quite forty – but –

There was a touch on his elbow, and he turned to find Bertram standing beside him. 'Chris, could you spare me two minutes?'

'Of course, Bertram. Come out on to the terrace.'

It was a fine warm night, but with a fair amount of cloud. As the moon came briefly from behind cover, Bertram gazed at the carefully tended grounds that stretched into the distance. In spite of his seemingly urgent request, he showed no inclination to speak, and Christopher had to prompt him.

'Yes. Sorry. I was thinking what a beautiful place you have here.'

'But that's not why you wanted to speak to me,' Christopher said tentatively.

'No, Chris, it's about these wretched attacks. They're so unnerving. One wonders what's going to happen next. The death of the dogs really shook me. I loved those animals, and to think that anyone – Peter White has confirmed it was rat poison.' Bertram turned away as if to hide his emotion.

'The police aren't being any use?' Christopher asked in an effort to return to practicalities.

'No, and I really can't blame them. I feel helpless myself, which is why I thought I'd consult you, ask if you had any bright ideas, if you could give me some advice. Chris, what would you do if you were in my position?'

'First, since the police are getting nowhere, I'd hire a private investigator. It seems to me that the guy who's responsible for what's been happening must be a local, or at any rate someone living not too far away, and it shouldn't be impossible to get a line on him.'

'That would cost a hell of a lot of money.'

'It wouldn't come cheap, but it might be worth it.'

'Any other suggestions?'

'As a preventive measure, yes. I would arrange for the grounds to be patrolled, if only for a few nights, and I'd make it known around that this was being done. It's easy enough to spread information in these parts – a word in the Windrush Arms, or a phone call to the *Courier*.'

'But it's not easy to provide such a guard. Daphne and I work hard all day. We need some sleep. And none of the men live in. I couldn't ask them to come back at night.'

'I could help.' Christopher had noticed that while Bertram had thought of Daphne, he had not mentioned Andrea. 'I'd be happy to do so, Bertram. I myself don't like the idea of some madman wandering around playing tricks. No one can feel safe.'

'It's very good of you, Chris, but –'

Bertram knew it was stupid to resent the offer, but he hated accepting favours, especially from Christopher. Yet he had asked for help, and he did have the women to consider, as well as himself. Probably Christopher was thinking of Andrea's safety, he thought bitterly.

'What kind of arrangement are you suggesting?' he asked.

'I could lend you a couple of my staff with their dogs. It would make no difference to them whether they're patrolling the grounds of the Hall or the Manor.'

'Do they do that every night?' Bertram asked in astonishment.

'No, not *every* night, though that's a secret between you and me, Bertram. In fact, at first it was almost every night, but now it's just a few nights a month at random. In fact, the Hall's reputation for security is high, and they've never had any trouble. It helps with the insurance. What do you say?'

'What can I say? All right, Chris. And many thanks.'

Supper was over. The guests had drifted back to the ballroom where the band had resumed playing, or were chatting in the drawing-room or on the terrace. An elderly couple, who had a long drive ahead, had already left for home. A waiter, one hired for the night, hurried up to Christopher.

'Sir, I was passing the library when the phone rang. The call is for a Miss Daphne, but I don't know who she is.'

'That's all right. I'll get her.'

He found Daphne on the terrace. 'Oh God!' she said. 'It must be Alice. No one else would phone me here at this time of night.'

'Let's hear what she has to say.'

It wasn't much, and it was confused. The old housekeeper had had a nightmare. She had woken, shaking with fear. She knew something was terribly wrong. She had dreamed there was a fire and she thought she could smell smoke through the window — somewhere outside. She babbled, appealing to Daphne to come.

'Alice, dear, I'll be with you as soon as I can. Put on your dressing-gown and wait for me in the hall. Switch all the lights on.'

Daphne turned to Christopher. 'I must go. I don't know what the trouble is, but she's frightened.'

'I'll fetch Bertram.'

'No. I can't wait, so don't worry him. You'll see that he and Andrea get home, won't you? I'll have to take the car.'

'Daphne, you can't go back to the Manor alone.'

'I must.'

She was at the door of the library and in the corridor outside half a dozen guests were admiring the modern paintings that lined the walls. They seized on their host, wanting to know more about the paintings and why he had chosen them. Daphne had disappeared before he was free.

Christopher cursed. He blamed himself. He told himself that Daphne was in no physical danger. If anyone had been trampling on the lettuces or pulling down the raspberry canes or letting the hens out again, the culprit would be long gone. Nevertheless, it wasn't right that Daphne should have been allowed to go off alone, even if it was to do no more than comfort the frightened old housekeeper. He was sure that, being a sensible woman, if there was real trouble at the Manor, she would telephone.

Christopher wandered among his guests, before stationing himself in the main hall. By now there was a steady trickle of departures, which increased as the band packed up. The party was over. He wished they would all go. He was more worried about Daphne than he cared to admit, and he had to make an effort to be the perfect host, saying farewells and accepting thanks, but he was used to dissembling his feelings.

'Daphne's gone ahead,' he said when Bertram and Andrea came to say goodbye. 'But Simon will drive you home.'

'Daphne? Why?'

'She'll explain.'

He waved a vague hand. Behind the Rocques were others waiting to express their thanks. First among them were Sir Philip Midvale and Lady Midvale. Philip Midvale was the chief constable of the Thames Valley Police Force, and Christopher Portman hoped that this wasn't an unfortunate omen.

10

Daphne was not as calm or self-composed as she had appeared. As she set off for Wychwood Manor, she knew she would have been glad of companionship, but waiting for Bertram, who would probably have demanded that Andrea should be told they were leaving and why, would have involved too many explanations and too much delay. Alice had sounded very upset, and it was not fair that the old woman should be subjected to such stress.

Daphne drove fast down the drive. On this special night the electronically-controlled gates stood open, and she was not held up. The two men on duty saluted her as she passed and she lifted a hand in acknowledgement. The lanes too were empty at this hour and she was able to maintain a good speed. She was soon close to the Manor, to home.

And she could smell smoke. She sniffed. It was wood-smoke, but woodsmoke mixed with something else, half-familiar but elusive. She turned into the entrance to the Manor and bumped quickly up the rutted drive, glad to see that Alice had turned on all the lights in the house, as she had been told.

The smell of burning was stronger now; the fire was obviously not in the house itself, but somewhere not far away. It would have to wait. Her first consideration must be for Alice. Daphne jumped out of the car and ran up the steps. The front door opened before she could rummage in her evening bag to get her key.

'Oh, Miss Daphne, I was waiting at the window, watching for you. Thank you for coming so quickly. It wasn't a night-mare, you know; at least not all of it was a dream. The smell of burning's real. A horrid smell. I've shut the bedroom windows, but it's seeping into the house.'

'Yes, it's horrid, but at least the fire, wherever it is, is outside. We don't have to worry about it immediately.' Daphne hoped this was true. She put her arms around Alice and gave her a hug. 'You're all right?'

'Now you're here, Miss Daphne, yes.'

'Good. Then you go into the kitchen and make us some tea. I've a torch in the car, and it's not very dark out. I'll try to discover what's burning.'

'But is it safe for you, Miss Daphne? Supposing he's still there – the vandal?'

'He won't be, Alice. If this is more of his work, he'll be well away by this time.'

Nevertheless, Daphne grasped the torch firmly, thankful that it was big and heavy and would, if necessary, be a means of defence. She went around to the back of the house. There was nothing to be seen, but the smell was stronger. She hesitated, wondering how far she should go. Then the clouds drifted from the face of the moon, and she thought she saw smoke rising from behind a small belt of trees that had been planted as a windbreak, but hadn't flourished.

She started to run, but the terrain was rough and the torch was growing dimmer, and she was forced to slow to a brisk walk. In any case, there was no reason for haste. She knew now what was burning. It was the old gazebo where, whatever the weather – in winter it could be heated by an oil stove – her mother had loved to write letters, and where she and Bertram and sometimes Christopher had played as children. But that was – what? Twenty-five – thirty years ago. At present the gazebo was almost derelict. The roof leaked, the door didn't shut properly and the formal gardens it had overlooked were no more. The once attractive little summerhouse was used only for storage.

As Daphne came in sight of it, the fire suddenly flared up and she saw the last wall collapse into the heap of charred wood which was all that remained of the structure. The smell here was strong, a stench, and she fumbled in her evening bag in search of a handkerchief; she had clung to the bag instinctively, perhaps because it contained her key to the house.

She recognized the smell now. It was the fertilizer which had been stored there, together with some odds and ends of garden equipment. Luckily, even if the gazebo and its contents were not covered by insurance, the loss was slight, and the house was quite safe; there was no chance the fire would spread to any other building or to any trees or bushes.

What mattered, she thought as she hurried back to the house, was that it was another attack by this unknown character who appeared determined to harry them, and them alone. No one else in the neighbourhood was suffering from his attentions. Wychwood Manor and its occupants were his sole target. Why? And it was so frustrating, for it seemed there was nothing they – or the police – could do about it.

Tea was ready by the time Daphne reached the kitchen. Alice had recovered from her fears but, as a kind of reaction, was eager to retell her experience, and to relate it to the burned-down gazebo. Daphne, who by now was feeling tired and dispirited, was forced to listen until she heard a car drive up; it was Simon Wayne bringing Bertram and Andrea. Simon came into the house with them, as Christopher had asked him to find out the nature of the trouble and make sure there was nothing he could do to help. Interminable explanations followed, and it was after four when finally she got to bed, and even then she found it difficult to sleep.

Christopher Portman arrived at the Manor shortly before noon. He gave as his excuse Daphne's mink jacket which she had left behind the previous evening, but he had other reasons. He wanted to hear at first hand the story of the night's alarms, and to see what problems there would be in guarding the property against an intruder.

As it was Sunday, there was little activity. In the early evening Bertram and Daphne would pick fruit to be taken to market the next day, but until then there wasn't much to do. Christopher found Bertram half asleep over the *Sunday Times*, Andrea mending the hem of a skirt that had become unstitched, and Daphne reading a book.

'What a domestic scene,' he mocked them, dropping Daphne's jacket on the sofa beside her.

'We're not fully awake,' Bertram said. 'It was a short night, even shorter than we had expected.'

'Yes. When Simon got back he told me what had happened. What he said was reassuring. Apparently, you'd had a fire in the old gazebo, without further damage. The work of the same villain who's got it in for you, I assume.'

'Presumably,' said Bertram. 'Some of the men go in there occasionally for a quiet smoke, but they wouldn't leave an empty can of petrol behind.' Bertram had been to inspect the charred remains earlier. 'I've phoned the police, but they're in no hurry to appear. Not that they'll achieve anything when they do.'

'It's very frightening.' Andrea looked up from her sewing. 'One doesn't know what might happen next.'

'With luck, nothing, darling.' Bertram was encouraging. 'I told you Chris is being kind enough to lend us a night watchman for a while. He'll patrol the grounds with his dog, and scare the damned chap off the scene if he comes, which probably he won't if he hears there's a guard on duty.'

'But we can't be guarded for ever,' Daphne protested. 'What's to prevent him waiting until he thinks it's safe, then having another go at us?'

'Don't be a pessimist, Daphne,' Christopher said firmly. 'Be practical instead. Come and show me round the place. It's ages since I had a good look and I want to gauge where you might be most vulnerable.' But, once outside, he said, 'You're right, of course. Until this guy is caught you're not going to feel really free of him.'

'It's horribly frustrating!' Daphne bent down and pulled up a weed with unnecessary force. 'We keep on asking why, and there's no answer. It makes it worse. Andrea's got a point. It *is* frightening to have to accept that there's some malignant character out there who hates us so much that he's prepared to – to go to such lengths to make our lives miserable.'

'I know. It's no fun, but cheer up.' Christopher put his arm around Daphne's shoulders comfortingly. 'Here's the poor old gazebo, or what's left of it.' He shook his head sadly. 'It brings back fond memories, doesn't it?'

Daphne didn't answer. She was wondering if Christopher remembered kissing her in the gazebo when she was fourteen and he a year older, the first time she had been kissed with anything that resembled passion. She doubted it.

'There's the petrol can,' she said coldly, pointing to a black battered object lying on the grass nearby.

'It wasn't there before?'

'Bertram says not.'

They wandered around the rest of the grounds, or what was left of them. Bertram had sold off as much as he could, and Christopher was secretly appalled, not only at the shrinkage of the estate, but also at its air of general neglect. Even the area devoted to the market garden looked shabby. The greenhouses needed a coat of paint, there was a broken trellis and unsuitable material had been flung on the compost heap, all small indications that the business was neither efficient nor flourishing.

'You've made a lot of changes since I saw around here last,' he said diplomatically to Bertram when he returned to the house with Daphne. 'But it shouldn't be too difficult to keep a watch over the essentials. I'll send Bill Crank along with Karl about nine. It will still be light, so he can familiarize himself with the place, and you can all meet him – and Karl, especially Karl. He's an ex-police dog, so he's trained to recognize friends and foes. Crank, incidentally, is an ex-police officer, invalided out of the force. He's not as quick as he was, but he's pretty competent.'

They thanked him. Bertram offered him a drink. Andrea pressed him to stay to lunch. He brushed their thanks aside, accepted a drink but refused lunch.

'I'm expecting a business phone call,' he lied.

'On Sunday?' said Andrea.

'Different countries, different customs.' He shrugged, eager now to get away.

Andrea saw him to the door, but she had time only to brush her lips against his and whisper, 'I'll phone. Make a date', before Alice came into the hall. Christopher, hoping that Alice hadn't seen the intimacy, called to her.

'Oh, Alice, I forgot to ask you. Last night, when you woke up, did you hear anyone or anything?'

Alice shook her head. 'No-o, sir. Nothing unusual. There was a motorcycle that backfired a couple of times, but that – that was all.'

'It was just an idea.'

Christopher waved a casual hand in goodbye to Andrea and smiled at Alice as she held open the door for him. But as he drove slowly down the drive his face was set in grim lines. He told himself it was absurd – innumerable people in the district owned motorbikes – but the moment Alice had mentioned hearing one backfiring about the time the gazebo was burning, he had thought of Gavin Brail, the man who had tried to blackmail him over Frankie Carton's death. Why? It was Bertram Rocque who was being persecuted, not Christopher Portman.

Four mornings later, Christopher Portman, going out to his car which was to take him to London, saw Bill Crank returning to Charlbury Hall after his night on guard at the Manor, and hailed him.

'Good morning, Bill. Any alarms or excursions?'

'Good morning, sir. Yes. The villain tried again last night. He doesn't read the *Courier* or go into any of the local pubs, or he'd know the Manor's heavily defended. We've spread the news, as you said to do, and the rumours have trebled the truth as usual. Karl and I have been made to sound like a full-blown platoon.'

Christopher shrugged. 'Alternatively, he's a determined man, and doesn't care a damn who might be waiting for him.'

'Oh, I'm not so sure about that, sir. He made off at speed when we came on him. He didn't want to be caught.'

'What happened exactly?'

'Well, sir, it was a few minutes after midnight. I'd made a circuit of the property and thought I'd take a gander at the greenhouses. I was just coming round the big one when Karl stopped suddenly. Then he growled deep in his throat and started to pull at his leash, and I knew we'd found trouble. But the moon came out and the chap saw us, and fled. I shouted at him to stop or I'd shoot, but he paid no attention and of course I didn't have a gun, not even a shotgun. I'm afraid he got clean away, sir.'

'That's OK, Bill. The main purpose of the exercise was to prevent him doing any more damage. If we had managed to identify him or learnt anything that would lead to his identification, it would have been an added bonus.'

'Well, he didn't do no harm, sir. We got to him in time. He dropped the big bottle of liquid weedkiller he was carrying and it was still full. It was strong stuff too, the kind you dilute with a lot of water.'

'Weedkiller?'

'Yes. I guess he meant to pour it into the rainwater butts. Sir Bertram was telling me he uses that water to mix the stuff to spray his fruit and veg with. I reckon the weedkiller wouldn't have done them much good.'

'No, indeed, it would not. Bill, you say you saw this man. Can you give any sort of description of him?'

'Not really, sir. Medium height, medium build, dressed in black with a stocking mask over his face. I suppose he pulled it off and stuffed it in his pocket before he got on his bike.'

'His bike?'

'Motorbike, sir. I heard it go off. It backfired a couple of times. Sorry I can't do better than that, sir.'

'You've done splendidly, Bill. Keep it up.'

'Yes, sir. Thank you, sir.'

The ex-policeman saluted as Christopher Portman nodded goodbye and went over to his car, where the chauffeur was patiently holding the door open for him.

He would have plenty of time to think about what Crank had said before he reached London and his thoughts were not pleasant. Clearly, his ruse to frighten off the villain by publicizing that the grounds of Wychwood Manor were being patrolled nightly had had no effect. What was more, the damned man seemed to be getting bolder – and therefore more dangerous. He had to be stopped, and not only stopped, but caught and punished before someone was badly hurt.

Christopher decided that, if Bertram didn't take any action, he would. He would appeal to Philip Midvale.

11

Two days later, Christopher arrived at Wychwood Manor at nine o'clock. Daphne, who had been up since six, was not at her best. She was wearing a dirty pair of jeans and a torn shirt. Her hair was dishevelled, her long face minus make-up, and there was a smear of dirt across her forehead. When Christopher, directed by Alice, eventually found her, she was on her knees, weeding a bed of onions, and she looked what she was – a tired, worried, unhappy woman, approaching middle age.

She was not welcoming. 'Hello, Chris. What is it? As you can see, I'm busy. Andrea's still in bed and Bertram's gone into Charlbury on business.'

'Hello, Daphne.' Christopher grinned at her. 'Daphne, I'm going on a comparatively extended trip to Europe. Not the usual fleshpots. Bulgaria, Hungary, places like that. However, I'll be in more or less daily contact with Simon, who'll be holding the fort in my absence. So if this joker continues to cause you any more trouble and you need personal help –'

'Thanks, Chris.' Daphne rocked back on her heels and brushed away her hair, spreading the dirt on her brow. 'I'll remember, but at the moment, as I said, Bertram's gone to Charlbury and I'm –'

'Busy weeding onions. Damn the onions! Daphne, I came over hoping to have a serious talk with you and I'm glad Bertram's not here. You're the most sensible person in this household.'

'Thanks!'

Christopher put out a hand and pulled Daphne to her feet. 'Come on, we can't talk here, among these vegetables.'

'Chris, it's nice to see you, but if you're thinking of this wretched persecution we've been suffering, is there anything to talk about? The local police are making inquiries though no one expects them to get anywhere. Your man Crank and his dog can't go on guarding us for ever, and anyway it's not a very satisfactory arrangement. Bertram's not happy about it.'

'That's precisely why something else has to be done.'

'What?'

They had been walking together away from the commercialized part of the grounds and were in sight of the scruffy piece of grass that had once been a fine lawn, overlooked by the main rooms of the house. It was here that sometimes on a summer's evening after work Bertram and Daphne and Andrea would sit, and there was a scattering of garden furniture. Now Christopher gestured towards it.

'Let's go and sit down and I'll tell you.'

'It's no use suggesting a private detective, as you did before, Chris. We can't afford it, and please don't offer to pay. Bertram would never accept, not even to protect Andrea.'

'I know. He's got the devil's own pride. Nevertheless, Daphne, this character's acts are becoming more and more spiteful. The attacks could easily become personal, as you must admit, and if they're allowed to go on one of you could get killed, which is a possibility that I don't view with any equanimity, I assure you,' Christopher snapped.

'Bertram has suggested that Andrea should go and stay with her sister for a while,' Daphne said coldly.

'What about you?'

'Chris, don't be stupid! I'm not Andrea.' Daphne found it impossible to keep the bitterness out of her voice. 'Besides, how could I leave Bertram to cope with the business? It's difficult enough anyway.'

'Yes, who would look after the onions?'

'Who indeed?'

They laughed together and the embarrassing moment, if it had been an embarrassing moment, passed. Neither of them, though for different reasons, wanted to talk of Andrea.

'OK, Daphne, let's be practical,' Christopher said. 'If you're to have any peace of mind, this individual who's becoming a real threat must be traced. A private detective is out. The local police are not capable and they won't want to appeal to their Headquarters. Anyway, you have to remember that the Thames Valley Police Force covers a wide area and is extremely busy. You can't expect them to pursue a phantom, even if Sergeant Donaldson could be persuaded to ask for help.'

'All right, Chris. You seem to have ruled out everything. What else is there?'

'String-pulling. A personal approach to the chief constable, Philip Midvale.'

'Bertram wouldn't do that. You know what he's like.'

'Yes, I know what he's like. He's prepared to get Andrea safely out of the way, but he thinks it fine that you should share the risks with him. But why should he endanger you? For that matter, why should he endanger himself? *Noblesse oblige?* You don't beg for favours if you're a baronet, like Sir Bertram Rocque. Is that it? Maybe in certain circumstances it's an admirable sentiment, but in this case it's pig-headed stupidity!'

Christopher Portman took several deep breaths. It wasn't often that he lost his temper and, when he did, it was nearly always deliberate and calculated. He glanced sideways at Daphne, who was staring straight in front of her. She had made no attempt to defend her brother, and Christopher would like to have known what she was thinking. He was indeed thankful that Bertram wasn't present.

'Then it's stalemate,' Daphne said at last. 'You'll never persuade Bertram.'

'I don't intend to try,' Christopher replied. 'I've already appealed to Midvale myself, but don't you dare tell that brother of yours.'

'Chris! What – what did the chief constable say?'

'He listened with great care, and he agreed that the present situation was fraught with danger, but –'

'Yes, but – he won't help? He'll wait till one of us is killed or badly hurt?'

'Daphne, be fair and wait till you hear what I have to say.

Midvale said he couldn't promise, but after some thought he asked if the name Tansey meant anything to me. Does it to you?'

Daphne frowned. 'Yes, I think so. Wasn't he the detective chief inspector who risked his life to save an autistic child from being kidnapped and used as a hostage? There was a lot of publicity about it.'

'That's right. Last year, in Colombury. He threw himself at a moving car. Anyway, he's spent ages in hospital, and as a result he's now on semi-sick leave, doing office work, which he hates. Midvale's going to ask him if he'll take on this investigation. Even the chief constable has to ask, because it's scarcely a job for a senior member of the Thames Valley Police Serious Crime Squad.'

'But that'll be wonderful, Chris, if he agrees.'

'It'll certainly relieve my mind about you all while I'm away, though Midvale reminded me that Tansey can't work miracles.'

While Christopher was explaining the situation to Daphne, Chief Inspector Dick Tansey had just entered the chief constable's office.

'Good morning, Chief Inspector,' Midvale greeted him. 'Lovely day.'

'Good morning, sir. Yes, indeed. Too lovely to waste.'

Midvale smiled broadly. He both liked and respected this tall, lean, good-looking man and he was well aware what his last remark had implied, but for the chief inspector's own sake he didn't want Tansey to return to active duty with the Serious Crime Squad until the medical people had passed him as fully fit again.

'Sir, I'm feeling fine and I was wondering –'

'Wait till you hear why I sent for you.'

'Yes, sir.' Tansey managed not to sigh.

'I want to ask you a favour. You can refuse if you like. You have every right to do so, as what I'm going to suggest is not strictly in your line of duty, or suitable for someone of your rank.'

Midvale shifted his heavy body in the chair that had been

specially made for him; even on a warm day like this his arthritis troubled him. 'At least it would take you away from your desk for a short while.'

'Sir, if that's so, you don't need to ask.'

'Don't be too sure. Now, you may have read or heard something about the troubles the people at Wychwood Manor are having, but unless the name ''Rocque'' meant anything to you, I doubt if you were interested, so I'll give you a brief outline of the matter. It came from a friend of mine − Mr Christopher Portman, who appealed to me for help, but whose name I don't want mentioned as my source. Only he, his colleague − a Mr Simon Wayne − and a Mrs Mariner − she's the sister of Sir Bertram Rocque − are to know why we are taking this sudden interest. It's like this, as far as I can make out . . .'

As the chief constable started to explain, Tansey's doubts grew. He understood why Sergeant Donaldson had been reluctant to appeal to Headquarters for assistance. Here was a series of fairly unimportant crimes with no definite connection between them, except that they all seemed to be aimed at this Sir Bertram Rocque and his family. None of them had had very serious consequences, but they were unpleasant, threatening − and gave the impression of being the work of a twisted mind. Moreover, the dangerous element in the crimes appeared to be on the increase.

When Midvale stopped speaking, saying that Sergeant Donaldson in Colombury would have all the files and presumably more detail, he asked Tansey's opinion. The chief inspector said, 'It strikes me that it's very much a matter for the local boys, sir. How would I explain my presence to Donaldson − after all, I'm fairly well known in the neighbourhood − or to anyone else who cares to ask? You say it's essential Mr Portman's name shouldn't be mentioned, and that only he and Mr Wayne and Mrs Mariner are aware how we became involved?'

'Yes. Sir Bertram would resent the interference − or at least the impression that he had pulled strings.'

'I understand,' said Tansey.

It was a conventional response, not meant to imply real

understanding. In fact, Tansey had no idea why Sir Bertram hadn't appealed directly to the chief constable, and it had been left to Portman to do so. However, one thing was clear to him. Midvale not only knew these people, but he knew far more about them than he was prepared to reveal to one of his chief inspectors.

'Sergeant Donaldson will be officially informed that you are taking over the inquiry,' Midvale said. 'He'll probably be glad to be rid of the problem, and anyway, he's in no position to query my decision. The same answer will do for everyone else: Headquarters are concerned at the number of unpleasant, potentially very dangerous incidents that have occurred in the district and intend to put a stop to them. Chief Inspector, in an ideal world, this would be true. The reason that it isn't is our lack of trained manpower.'

'I appreciate that, sir.'

There was a silence. Tansey hesitated. He wanted to say that he would gladly accept the assignment. It was obviously what the old man was hoping for. But he wasn't sure that he was ready to return to Colombury – the scene of his last case, the one that had resulted in that long stay in hospital. Then he thought of his stuffy office, and how pleasant it would be to drive into the country with a gentle breeze blowing through the windows of the car.

'Dick, forget any idea about doing me a favour. You don't have to take this on if you don't want to. It's entirely up to you.' The use of Tansey's first name was confirmation that Midvale meant what he said.

'I know, sir.' Without more thought Tansey made up his mind. 'Of course I'll take it on.'

'Good!'

As Tansey left the office, the chief constable was smiling. He had made no promises to Christopher Portman, and indeed had been on the point of refusing his request, albeit regretfully. The Thames Valley Force, what with holidays, sick leave and the rash of extra crimes that summer always spawned, was hopelessly understaffed. Then he had thought of Detective Chief Inspector Tansey.

Philip Midvale made a point of knowing all his senior staff, and by chance he had got to know Dick Tansey better than most officers of his rank. He was fully aware of how much Tansey hated being deskbound, and was fretting to return to the Crime Squad but, according to his medical reports, he was not yet fully ready for the change. Now, Midvale congratulated himself, he had found a job for Tansey which would take him out of the office but shouldn't be too taxing, and he had done a favour to Portman, who was a casual friend and almost a neighbour. As he reached for the telephone to inform Christopher Portman that one of his senior officers, the Detective Chief Inspector Tansey whom he had mentioned, would be conducting some preliminary inquiries, the chief constable considered that it had been a good morning's work.

Back in his own office, Tansey consulted his small reference library. He had got the impression from the chief constable that his assignment was not to be publicized in the Headquarters, though he could expect reasonable support, and for a start a copy of *Who's Who* was all he needed. He looked up Portman first. He smiled to himself; he was always surprised how much could be learnt from these potted autobiographies, not only from what was included, but from what was omitted. For anyone who read them perceptively they were often extraordinarily revealing and, as an intelligent man, Tansey found them both amusing and informative.

His mini-research completed, he then phoned Sergeant Donaldson in Colombury to make sure he would be available that morning. To his surprise, he found that the chief constable's office had already been in touch with the sergeant, and that the latter was only too ready to cooperate. This was welcome news.

But he was slightly annoyed, on reaching the police station in Colombury, to find that Donaldson was not there. An apologetic constable explained that a serious accident had occurred at one of the farms, a man had been crushed under a tractor, and the sergeant had thought it his duty to attend. However, the constable produced the relevant files and Tansey, seated at Donaldson's desk, got down to work.

When the sergeant returned, he briefed the chief inspector on what he knew, and expanded on the contents of the files, which had been maintained meticulously. To give him his due, Donaldson, although somewhat unappealing in his manner, was a good police officer, Tansey thought.

Donaldson finally commented, 'You see that we were first called in when the Toyota was vandalized at the railway station, sir.'

'Yes.' Tansey was frowning. 'And there seems to be a slight discrepancy about that. The porter says he saw the Toyota had been damaged when he went for his dinner break at twelve o'clock, but apparently on her return from London that evening Lady Rocque didn't notice, although she got as far as trying to start the car. Did you query this, Sergeant?'

'Not with Lady Rocque, sir. I saw nothing to be gained by it.' Donaldson looked uncomfortable; he hadn't been prepared to question her ladyship.

'Have you had many dealings with her?' Tansey was curious.

'If you mean is she well known to the police, no, sir. She's been caught for speeding a couple of times. Nothing serious. The second occasion her ladyship was fined quite heavily, but she didn't complain.'

Bully for her, Tansey thought, amused by Donaldson's attitude. 'Perhaps you'd put a call through to Wychwood Manor for me, Sergeant. I want to make an appointment to interview the Rocques this afternoon.'

'Of course, sir.'

Bertram answered the phone himself. He had just returned from Charlbury, where his business had not gone well, and he was not in the best of tempers. He flatly refused to see the chief inspector, saying that he was too busy and he couldn't imagine what good it would do or why there was this sudden interest in his affairs at the Thames Valley Police Headquarters.

Tansey, at his tactful best by being a little less than truthful, managed to placate him and it was agreed that the chief

106

inspector would call at Wychwood Manor the following morning.

By now it was too late to attempt anything else before lunch. Tansey had a quick sandwich and a half pint at the Windrush Arms, and drove to the railway station.

Surprisingly, the car park was nearly full, for Colombury was not the busiest of stations, though a fair number of trains went through each day without stopping. He guessed that many of the cars belonged to shoppers from the outlying villages, or to visitors. There was no guard on the parked vehicles.

He found the porter he wanted without difficulty. His name was Alf Jones, and he confirmed the story he had told Sergeant Donaldson; the Toyota had been damaged before midday.

'Why didn't you report it?'

'Not my business, sir. Look at the notice: Cars parked at the owner's risk.'

'Were you on duty when the London train came through that evening?' Tansey asked.

Alf Jones nodded. 'And it was me what helped Lady Rocque with her parcels. She gave me a pound tip. Very generous, it was.' He grinned, showing a missing front tooth.

'You had tried to start the Toyota for her. Why didn't you point out the damage that had been done to it then?'

Alf Jones looked puzzled. 'I didn't try to start it for her. I didn't know it was her Toyota. She asked me for a taxi and I carried her parcels out to one. There's usually a couple what meets that London train. The next day Mr Field from the Windrush Garage came to take the car away, and he sent for the police because of the vandalism. He said the car belonged to Sir Bertram Rocque. Before that I hadn't connected it with him or Lady Rocque. Why should I?'

Why indeed, Tansey thought. This was a different version of the story from the one that Lady Rocque had given Donaldson and her husband. Why had she bothered to lie?

'I don't understand,' he said, almost to himself. 'If Lady Rocque didn't go to her car after she got off the train, how did she know it wouldn't start?'

'Search me! It started like a bird next morning when Mr Field tried. Mind you, I think it was sensible of her to leave it here overnight in the circs.'

'What circs?'

Jones took off his cap and scratched his head. 'I don't want to say anything against the lady. Obviously she'd been having a fine day in London, plenty of expensive shopping, probably a good lunch with friends, but a bit too much to drink.'

'Are you saying she was drunk?'

'Not drunk, no. But she'd been drinking, all right. You could smell her breath, and she was a little unsteady on her feet. Just merry, I'd call it, but it wouldn't have been wise to drive.'

'That's probably why she took a taxi, then.'

Silently blessing the garrulous porter, Tansey thanked him and went to collect his own car. And now what? Before his nine-to-five office job at Headquarters, he would never have dreamed of abandoning his inquiries at this point. He would probably have called on ex-Sergeant Court, Donaldson's predecessor and a mine of information about the neighbourhood. Today, however, remembering that Hilary, his wife, would be expecting his return at what had become his usual time, he set off for Kidlington. But he couldn't help feeling amused at his pangs of guilt.

12

Hilary Tansey had received her husband's news with equanimity. If she had any doubts about his fitness, she hid them from him. He was clearly so pleased and, for the first time in months so eager next morning to go to work, that she had to be happy for him. Promising to telephone if he was to be late home, Dick Tansey left the house, waving his usual goodbye. Their life, Hilary thought ruefully, had reverted to normal.

As soon as he reached his office, Tansey phoned ex-Sergeant George Court, now retired. Tansey liked Court and had got on well with him. When Court had been in charge of the Colombury police station, Court had been slow and painstaking, but competent enough and, most important, always ready to appeal to Headquarters rapidly for assistance if necessary. However, as the market town had grown, the pressure on the local police had grown too, and Court had been glad to retire and give way to a probably more efficient but considerably less popular man.

Court greeted Tansey warmly. 'Chief Inspector, sir, how nice to hear your voice. How are you?'

'Not too bad. Still on semi-sick leave. But I'm looking into an affair in your neighbourhood, and I hoped I might come along and have a chat with you. Get some background information.'

'You mean the funny goings-on at Wychwood Manor?'

Tansey laughed. 'I've obviously reached the right man.'

'I don't know about that, sir, but you're very welcome. I'll tell you what the local gossip says, for what it's worth, and what's been in the *Courier* – though I expect they've kept the clippings on file at the station.'

Tansey thanked him, and promised to be along in the course of the morning. Next, he tried Mr Christopher Portman who, through his friendship with the chief constable, had instigated the inquiry, and therefore, in Tansey's book, had some considerable interest in the matter – though evidently not enough to keep him at home. Mr Portman, Tansey was informed, was abroad and would not be returning to England for several days.

So Tansey departed for Colombury and George Court. The Courts lived in one of the council houses on what had once been the outskirts of the town, but had now been absorbed by it. Nevertheless, their house, like all the others in the row, had a comparatively large back garden, and it was here, sitting in comfortable chairs on a neat lawn, that the two men caught up with their mutual news.

'Well, enough of this nostalgia. I mustn't keep you chatting, Chief Inspector. You're still a busy man,' said Court as his wife brought out the two early cups of coffee she had insisted on making for them. 'But if it's these strange incidents at Wychwood Manor you're interested in, I'm not sure I can help a lot. I don't really know much more than what I've learnt from the media and, as always, except for the *Courier* chap, they lost interest quickly.'

'I think you may be able to help. First, tell me about the Rocques and Mrs Mariner. Are they popular characters locally?'

'I'd have said that Sir Bertram is very popular. I've never heard anything said against him. Oh, he's no businessman – I guess his market garden business runs at a loss – and he does owe money around, but he's not mean, and when he was forced to get rid of staff he went out of his way to try to find other jobs for them. His popularity makes these attacks on him all the more difficult to understand.'

'Is there any chance that Lady Rocque could be the object of the attacks?'

'I shouldn't think so,' Court said slowly, and added with

a wide smile, 'Not unless the wife of one of her smart friends is feeling particularly jealous.'

Tansey returned the smile with a grin. 'You'll have to elaborate on that last remark, George.'

'Sir – perhaps I've said too much.' Court was embarrassed.

'Nonsense! Of course you haven't – said too much, I mean. That's why I'm here, to pick up gossip. And for heaven's sake stop calling me sir. You're not in the force any more, George.'

'No – I mean yes.' Court swallowed the sir; old habits died hard. 'About Lady Rocque. She's a very beautiful lady, very attractive, the sort that turns every man's head when she comes into a room.'

'Even yours?'

'Mine?' Court snorted. 'She wouldn't look at the likes of me. She prefers them rich and good-looking, like Mr Portman of Charlbury Hall.'

'Portman?' Tansey was surprised. 'I thought perhaps Portman and Mrs Mariner –'

'No, sir! I think not.'

Court went on to explain the complex relationship, as it was generally accepted, that existed between Bertram and Andrea Rocque, Daphne Mariner, and Christopher Portman. And Tansey wondered why Andrea Rocque had remained, if not faithful to an impoverished husband, lacking in glamour, at least still with him, presumably doing her wifely duties. For that matter, why had she married him in the first place?

'I don't know,' Court said, when asked. 'She might have liked the idea of being Lady Rocque of Wychwood Manor. When they were married about ten years ago, old Sir David had just died, but Bertram's mother was alive – she was killed soon afterwards in a hunting accident – and the estate was altogether more flourishing then than it is today. Besides, I did hear that, beautiful as Andrea Rocque is, she wasn't much of an actress, so perhaps she didn't fancy continuing with a career that wasn't a great success.'

'Where was Mrs Mariner during this time?'

'At the Manor. Her marriage only lasted about a year, and

she came home. I've no idea why, or what happened to Mariner, but I do know there was a divorce eventually.'

'It happens in the best of families,' Tansey said lightly, thinking of his own first marriage. 'George, I must go. Thank you for all the information you've given me. You're a positive encyclopædia. And thank Mrs Court for the coffee.'

As Tansey drove to Wychwood Manor and his appointment with Sir Bertram Rocque, he reflected on all that George Court had told him. He accepted that most of it was gossip, but that didn't mean it was valueless. On the contrary, often gossip proved extremely useful, and a trifling piece of information could help solve a case. Besides, he always liked to understand the background of the people involved.

On his arrival, in spite of Court's warning that the Rocques were no longer rich, the ill-kept drive was a surprise that only partially prepared him for the clearly impoverished condition of the estate. However, Sir Bertram himself came up to expectations. He was almost a caricature of a country gentleman, with neat leather patches on the elbows and around the cuffs of what had once been an expensive tweed jacket. And, slightly ashamed of his abruptness the day before on the telephone, he was friendly, not in the least patronizing, and almost apologetic to be the cause of so much trouble to the police.

'I'm surprised to see you, Chief Inspector,' he said. 'I thought that Sergeant Donaldson had decided not to seek assistance.'

Tansey made a non-committal reply, and Sir Bertram went on. 'As you said on the phone, you've come about these damnable so-called incidents.'

'Yes, sir.'

Sir Bertram said, 'In the beginning, the incidents were annoying, but not really important. They were certainly not important enough to warrant your attention, Chief Inspector – in fact, I'm not sure they are now – though I admit to being shaken when my dogs were poisoned. And of course, we had no idea that these attacks – if you can call them that – would continue. They've upset my wife horribly.'

'Really, sir? I would hope to speak to Lady Rocque when it's convenient.'

'Not now. She's still in her room. She woke up with a headache this morning.'

'I see. Well, perhaps you'd be good enough, sir, to tell me in your own words exactly what happened.'

'Of course. It was like this –' For the third time that day, Tansey found himself listening to the now familiar recital.

When Sir Bertram had come to an end, Tansey said, 'You believe one person is responsible for all these incidents, sir?'

'I just don't know! The vandalism of the Toyota at the railway station could be unrelated. But I don't know! I don't know what to believe, Chief Inspector, and, before you ask me, I've no enemies that I'm aware of. I run a market garden with my sister, and I lead a very quiet life.'

'What about any business rivals, sir?'

Bertram Rocque's tired face broke into a grin. 'My dear Chief Inspector, if you knew the state of my business you wouldn't ask that. Except for my immediate family, it wouldn't matter a damn if we folded tomorrow.'

'What about employees? Have you sacked anyone who might bear a grudge?'

'No-o –'

Tansey noted the slight hesitation before Rocque's answer, but he didn't have time to pursue the matter. A shadow had fallen across the worn carpet as a woman came through the French windows into the room. There was no need for the introduction which Bertram Rocque performed. Seen beside him, it was obvious that this was his sister, Daphne Mariner. She was wearing jeans and an old silk shirt, comfortable, workaday clothes and, when she shook hands, Tansey felt the hard, rough skin. Clearly Mrs Mariner was more than a sleeping partner in the market garden business.

'Chief Inspector,' she said, 'I'm afraid my brother told you a little white lie just now. He recently sacked a man called David Garson, who was his assistant here.'

'I didn't sack him. He went of his own accord.'

'After we caught him fiddling the books. He must have cheated us out of a couple of hundred pounds, if not more.'

'All right! But he was ashamed of what he'd done, and said he bitterly regretted it. I'm sure he wouldn't dream of – of the kind of persecution that this character is apparently attempting.'

'Do you know where Garson is now?' asked Tansey.

'He's working in Oxford, I think. I gave him a good reference. Apart from this one aberration he was fine.'

Seeing Sir Bertram's mouth set in a thin line, Tansey decided to leave the subject of David Garson for the moment. After all, as far as the chief inspector was concerned, this was only the opening skirmish in the affair, and Garson could easily be a red herring. He changed the subject dramatically.

'Sir Bertram, I must ask you this question. If you were to die, who would inherit?'

'Inherit? Oh, you mean the title, the estate. I have no children. A distant cousin in New Zealand would become the next baronet, but he wouldn't get anything else. The property's not entailed or anything of that kind. My estate, which unfortunately doesn't amount to much at present, will go to my wife after a few small gifts. But I don't expect to die yet awhile, Chief Inspector.'

'I sincerely trust not, sir.'

Tansey made the conventional reply. He saw Rocque glance at his watch and knew that he was outstaying his welcome. There were still a great many questions he needed to ask and he would have to talk to Daphne Mariner alone at some point, but he sensed that now was not the right moment. He suggested that Sir Bertram should walk around the grounds with him, and show him the sites of the incidents. He didn't expect to learn much from them, but he hoped that Rocque would be more relaxed out of doors. First, he was shown the henhouse, then the greenhouses, the field where the horses grazed and the place where the two dogs had eaten the rat poison.

Bertram Rocque, who had been fairly silent so far during the tour, restricting his remarks to facts and offering no opinions, finally turned to Tansey and said, 'You know, Chief Inspector, it's the poisoning of the dogs that has disturbed me most. I think it was because of them – the idea that anyone was prepared to kill two such lovely animals for his own secret purpose – that I accepted Mr Portman's offer to let this man, Crank, come here at night as a guard. But I'm not sure it was a good idea.'

'Why not?'

'Because he scared the joker away from the Manor.' Rocque pointed to the charred remains of the gazebo. 'That was the last effort in the grounds, but I'm afraid he might try something different, a personal attack perhaps.'

Tansey thought for a moment. 'You say, sir, that the joker, as you call him, hasn't come since you had a guard, but I understood –'

'No, no, I didn't. He did come, just once after the news that the place was patrolled was spread. Perhaps he hadn't yet heard about the guard.' Rocque shrugged. 'I don't know. Anyhow, Crank and his dog chased him away.'

'Please tell me about it.'

Rocque explained that Crank had only seen a shadowy figure, who had fled, probably on a motorbike. But he went on to say that Alice Marsh, the housekeeper at the Manor, believed that she'd heard a motorbike the night the gazebo was burnt down. This was news to Tansey.

'You didn't tell the police about this, sir?' he said.

'I gave Donaldson the weedkiller the man had hoped to put in my watering system, but I didn't mention the sound of the motorbike. No. What was the point?' Rocque shrugged. 'Donaldson couldn't check all the motorbikes in the district, and anyway, it's almost certainly a coincidence.'

Tansey kept his thoughts to himself. Rocque could be right. Certainly it could be coincidence, but he would have to talk to Crank and to the Rocques' housekeeper. However, they could wait. By now he and Rocque had returned to the house, and Rocque clearly had no intention of asking him in again. He thanked Rocque and took his leave.

On his return to Kidlington, Tansey turned to the Oxford telephone directory. Several Garsons were listed, but on the third attempt the phone was answered by a woman who said Tansey must mean her husband's nephew. She provided a phone number and the address of his place of work, and, after lunch in the mess, Tansey telephoned Garson at his office and asked if he would be free for half an hour that afternoon. Garson was obviously startled by the request.

'I don't understand, Chief Inspector,' he said. 'Why should you want to talk to me about Sir Bertram Rocque's affairs?'

'You may be able to help me, Mr Garson. Shall I come along to your office, or would you prefer to meet at our Kidlington headquarters?'

There was an appreciable pause while Garson pondered the alternatives. 'My office – if it's not inconvenient for you.'

'Fine. About three o'clock. Shall I say that Mr Tansey has an appointment with Mr Garson?'

'Thank you. I'll book us a room.' Garson's voice was tight, appreciative of the fact that he wouldn't have to make up some story to explain to the receptionist the reason for a visit from a police chief inspector.

And when Tansey arrived at the large estate offices over a shop in Oxford's Broad Street, he was shown into a small conference room as if he were a prospective client. David Garson was a surprise. For some reason Tansey had imagined him to be around forty, a big man with a weather-beaten face. In fact, Garson was the reverse. Still in his twenties, he was a pale, indoor type with thick spectacles. He pulled out a chair for Tansey.

'You surprised me this morning, Chief Inspector,' he said, 'but I've had time to think, and it's obvious why you want to see me. You believe I may be responsible for the unpleasant incidents that have been happening to the Rocques because I was – was forced to leave my job at the Manor. I assure you that I've had nothing whatsoever to do with them. And I'd hate Sir Bertram to think that I had. He was very generous to me.'

'You don't bear him any malice for sacking you?' Tansey asked bluntly.

'No, why should I? I was a fool. I got into financial diffi-culties and fiddled the market garden books. I meant to pay the money back, but Mrs Mariner caught me out first.'

'Do you hold a grudge against Mrs Mariner then?'

'No. She was in the right, and it taught me a lesson. I might have gone on fiddling – stealing to give it its proper name – if I'd not been caught.'

'But you must regret losing your old job, Mr Garson. It was pleasant living at the Manor, wasn't it?'

'The job was fine, but I didn't live at the Manor, Chief Inspector. I lived in digs in Colombury and went backwards and forwards on my motorbike. Good digs they were, too – much better than the ones I've got here at present.'

'Do you ever go back to Colombury?'

'Yes. Luckily, as an estate agent it's part of the work to get out of the office – to inspect properties or show clients around – and if I'm near Colombury I call on my ex-landlady. She's an old dear. She keeps me up to date with the local gossip.'

Tansey had no more questions. Garson had volunteered everything he wanted to know, and had shown himself to be a perfect suspect. But there was a long way to go yet, Tansey was sure, though he was not dissatisfied with his day's work.

13

It was the next day. The weather was beautiful and Bertram Rocque took his time strolling down to the field where the horses grazed. He leaned on the gate and regarded them fondly. The family had always kept horses, and he was loath to part with them, but he knew they were a wild extravagance.

In the summer they were more or less self-supporting, but in the winter they needed stabling and fodder, and there were the occasional vet's bills. He couldn't afford them. It wasn't as if he and Daphne hunted any longer – there were too many incidental expenses connected with hunting – and Andrea, who would have loved the social side of the sport, was no more than an average horsewoman, and always would be, in spite of the many lessons she continued to have.

Bertram smiled to himself. Passionately as he loved Andrea, he had few illusions about her, and he knew that her visits to the riding school were not so much to improve her equestrian ability as to meet people, to make new friends, to widen her circle of acquaintances. If some of these were characters he didn't particularly care for, it didn't matter; though he was occasionally included in the invitations she received, Andrea didn't expect him to accompany her. It was an admirable arrangement and, though sometimes he couldn't avoid the odd pang of jealousy, he still didn't blame her.

He caught Mollie, the roan mare, put a leading rein on her and led her from the field; the other two horses had lost interest. He would sell them, he decided. Daphne wouldn't mind. But he would keep old Mollie for Andrea; the riding school encouraged pupils to bring their own horses if they possessed them.

Andrea was waiting when Bertram reached the stables, and he thought how elegant she looked in hacking jacket and jodhpurs. He saddled the mare for her, and gave her a leg-up before handing her her whip.

'I wish I were coming with you, darling. I could do with a ride this morning, but I can't get away from here. There's too much to be done.'

'No, you don't, Bertram. You'd be bored stiff.'

'I expect you're right.' He gave her a loving smile and patted the mare on the rump. 'Take care, Andrea. Don't trot on the hard road. Walk. You've plenty of time.'

'OK.'

Andrea saluted him with her whip and he watched her move off down the drive before going along to the greenhouses. He wasn't worried about her. She was reasonably competent and careful, and most of the way to the riding school, which was not far from the Manor, was on field paths or at worst grass verges. Only a quarter of a mile was on an open road.

'Andrea, lovely to see you, as always.'

'And you, Marlene.'

The two ladies rode into the yard of the Drivers' riding school side by side. Mrs Sinclair was one of the friends Andrea had met at the school early the previous year, almost at once to receive an invitation to the marriage of the Sinclairs' son to Sally-Ann Jowett. Andrea had no delusions. She knew that she had been taken up by Marlene Sinclair because she had a title and was the wife of a baronet, Sir Bertram Rocque, whose family had lived at Wychwood Manor for generations. She didn't mind. The Sinclairs were rich and, eager to establish themselves in the district, gave a lot of parties which Andrea enjoyed. Moreover, Marlene was always ready to provide her with an alibi, when one was needed.

'And how is dear Chris?' Marlene Sinclair asked.

Andrea resented the question and its implication, but she

didn't show her pique. She merely said, 'Fine, as far as I know. Flown off on some mysterious business jaunt, as usual.'

Their conversation was interrupted by more arrivals in the yard, two on their own mounts, and three who had driven up to the school together in a Range Rover. The Drivers' man brought out horses, already saddled, and Andrea was aware that beside the other animals, poor old Mollie looked what she was, an elderly badly-groomed mare. She determined that next week she would persuade Bertram to let her ride one of his better horses.

This decision was strengthened as the morning progressed. It was a disappointment when, instead of the handsome and flirtatious Rodney, who had been called up for jury duty, Audrey, his short dumpy wife, appeared to take the lesson. And with Audrey in charge it was a true lesson, not merely an amble through the woods with a few canters around a field. Audrey schooled them over jumps for more than an hour, giving each rider individual criticism. It was not what most of them enjoyed, certainly not Andrea, who found it boring and tiring, especially as Mollie appeared equally bored and made no attempt to collaborate.

It had been an unpleasant morning, Andrea decided, as she rode out of the school. Audrey Driver had been far from complimentary about her riding. One of her companions had commiserated with her on her 'poor old mare', and suggested she would do better on a horse belonging to the school. The only cheering occurrence had been an invitation to lunch with Marlene Sinclair the following week.

Andrea waved to Marlene as their ways parted. She was accepting too much hospitality from the Sinclairs, she thought angrily, but what else could she do? She and Bertram entertained very little, and anyway, he didn't like the Sinclairs. To relieve her feelings she gave Mollie a sharp flick of the whip on the rump. The mare paid no attention whatsoever.

'You silly beast!' she said aloud.

She glanced at her watch. If she hurried there would be just time to get home, shower, change her clothes and have a drink before lunch. She could do with a stiff drink. She dug in her heels, but the mare refused to respond and they jogged along steadily. She would have hit the animal again, but by now they had reached a stretch of tarmac road where there were no grass verges. A car overtook them, and a couple of cyclists. A van, going in the opposite direction, passed. Andrea kept well in to the side, but the placid Mollie showed no interest, though, sensing that she would soon be home, she quickened her pace a little.

Chief Inspector Tansey arrived at Wychwood Manor without warning. He had hoped to interview Lady Rocque and was disappointed to hear that she had gone for her riding lesson.

'Not that they'll ever make a horsewoman out of her.' Alice sniffed. 'She's not got the seat or the hands, not like Miss Daphne.'

Thinking it was obvious where the housekeeper's affections lay, Tansey said, 'Where is Miss Daphne – Mrs Mariner? Perhaps I could have a word with her.'

'Working, as usual – down by the greenhouses, sir.'

'And Sir Bertram?'

'He's in the office, telephoning.'

'I'll go and see Mrs Mariner then. But first, Alice, will you tell me about the night the gazebo was burnt down. I'd like to hear the story from you personally.'

There wasn't much, and Alice added nothing to what Tansey already knew. But she reiterated that she had heard a motorbike, which was unusual at that time of night.

'It backfired,' she said, 'just as the one Mr Crank heard some nights later when he nearly caught the man, though I must admit I didn't associate it with the intruder at the time, not until I was talking with Mr Crank.'

'That's very interesting,' Tansey said.

He thanked her and, following her directions, went off to find Daphne who, swathed in a large gardener's apron, was washing out flowerpots under an outside tap. It was a messy job, and she didn't look as if she were enjoying it.

'Hello, Chief Inspector,' she said wearily.

'Hello, Mrs Mariner. I can see you're busy, but could you

121

spare me a few minutes? There are some questions I'd like to ask you.'

'Sure. I'd be glad of a rest. Shall we sit on the wall over there?'

Tansey followed Daphne and perched on the stone wall beside her. 'Mrs Mariner,' he began, 'Sir Philip Midvale, my chief constable, told me that neither Sir Bertram nor Lady Rocque knows that, since the local police didn't seem to be getting anywhere, Mr Portman had appealed to him to instigate a more serious inquiry into your troubles here, but that you know about Mr Portman's intervention.'

'That's right. My brother hates asking favours. It's silly of him, but there you are, and Chris – Mr Portman – is a very old friend. We've known each other since the three of us – Bertram, Christopher and myself – were children. Then Mr Portman went away and got very rich. We stayed here and got pretty poor.'

Daphne smiled ruefully and Tansey returned her smile. He liked her. She had no pretensions, and he noticed that she had said nothing about Portman having been the son of the Rocques' head gardener.

'You know, Chief Inspector, these incidents, or whatever one calls them, are frightening. It's dreadful to think there's someone who hates us so much that he wants to hurt us. And he has hurt us. He's cost us a lot of money, and those poor hens and the dogs – that was revolting!' Daphne shuddered. 'You must find him, Chief Inspector, before he does something worse.'

'I'll do my best, Mrs Mariner. I suppose you haven't *any* idea who it might be? What about Mr Mariner? I gather you're not on the best of terms with your husband.'

Daphne Mariner turned towards Tansey. 'My dear Chief Inspector, I'm sorry. I mustn't laugh, but – you can't suspect poor Stewart. It wouldn't have been his line at all. He'd have come, full of charm, in a hired Rolls, wanting a large loan.'

'You speak of him in the past tense.'

'Yes, he's dead. His brother, who's a perfectly respectable lawyer in Edinburgh, wrote and told me. Stewart died of an overdose of sleeping pills after half a bottle of whisky about

122

eight years ago. No one knows if it was deliberate or not. I have to admit I didn't shed a tear.'

'You hadn't had a happy marriage?'

'No. It lasted less than a year, and I came home to Mother.' Daphne gave a wry smile. 'It was my own fault. I married Stewart out of pique, when I heard that the man I was in love with had married someone else. Ironically, this turned out not to be true, but I was eighteen at the time and – and not as sensible as I hope I am now. But enough of my past, Chief Inspector. You can certainly rule Stewart out of your inquiries.'

'So it would seem. But what about David Garson, then? It was you, I gather, who caught him fiddling the accounts. Might he not bear you a grudge?'

'I very much doubt it. I was angry at the time. We could ill afford the loss of the money, but we parted on reasonably good terms. In fact, Bertram was overly generous to him. No, Chief Inspector, I've given the matter some serious thought and I regret having mentioned his name. I'm sure he's not the culprit. For one thing, he's got a good job in Oxford. Why risk it? And why wait five or six months after he was sacked?'

Those, Tansey thought, are two pertinent questions. Why should anyone take the risk of being caught, and the possible consequences? Either the culprit considered it worthwhile, or he was being very well paid. And why now? Something fairly recent must have triggered off these attacks, not something that had happened months ago. If I could answer those two questions, Tansey decided, the file on the case might be nearer to closure.

'Honestly, Chief Inspector, I haven't any idea who it might be,' Daphne continued. 'Somehow that makes it worse, not better. I –' She stopped abruptly and slid off the wall where they had been sitting. 'Here's Bertram! He's running. Something's wrong.'

Bertram was out of breath when he reached them. He ignored Tansey's presence. 'I – I have to go to Colombury – to the hospital,' he said. 'It's Andrea. Dr Band just phoned.

He says she's unconscious. They don't know yet how – how bad she is, but that I should come.'

'Yes, of course. But what happened, Bertram? Was Andrea taken ill?'

'No one quite knows. It seems Mollie bolted just along the road not far from here, and went straight into a car. An accident – horrible.'

'Mollie – bolted? That's absurd! Why –'

'For God's sake, stop asking questions, Daphne. I don't know the answers. I'll phone you from the hospital when I do.'

'All right, but take care, Bertram. It won't help Andrea if you drive into a ditch.'

Bertram didn't acknowledge the remark. Daphne doubted if he had heard it. He was on his way, his only thought to get to Andrea as soon as possible. Daphne could understand his feelings. If it had been Christopher – or even Bertram himself – she would have felt the same. Christopher? If Andrea had been badly hurt, was dying, he would want to know, to be with her. For a split second Daphne pictured Bertram and Christopher, one on either side of Andrea's death bed, like a scene remembered from a Victorian painting or an old movie. Then she became aware that Tansey was repeating a question.

'Mrs Mariner, I must go, but first why did you say it was absurd that the horse should have bolted?'

'Because Mollie's a poor old thing. She needs a lot of persuasion even to canter, and though Andrea's no horsewoman she's not stupid. She wouldn't do anything foolish. I don't understand – Oh God!' Involuntarily Daphne seized Tansey by the arm. 'Chief Inspector, you don't think it's – it's another "incident", that somehow Mollie was made to bolt?'

'I don't know, Mrs Mariner.' Gently, Tansey released his arm. 'I'm going to find out. I suggest you go inside the house and make yourself a strong drink. You may have a long wait ahead before there's any news.'

The chief inspector had no difficulty in finding the scene of the accident. The entire local police force from the Colombury station seemed to be scattered around a Jaguar which was obstructing the road, though it was far from obvious what they were doing. They appeared to be waiting and, as Tansey sighted Sergeant Donaldson and made towards him, the reason became clear.

There was the report of a rifle shot, causing some rooks in a nearby tree to fly into the air. Then, as the echo died, a heavy silence fell, while everything and everyone momentarily stood still – before once more the film was restarted.

Tansey came around to the front of the Jaguar, where the lifeless remains of the old roan mare were draped over the bonnet. A man in a brown, linen-like coat over his clothes was checking the rifle, ready to put it away. Another man in an elegant blood-spattered suit had run to the edge of the road and was vomiting into the ditch; Sergeant Donaldson introduced Tansey to the first man, who turned out to be Peter White, the local vet and indicated that the second was Tom Richardson, a lawyer, the owner of the Jaguar. There were two photographers, one of them a plain-clothes policeman, the other from the *Courier*. A couple of men were starting to take measurements. There was a great deal of blood in the road and a disgusting stench that Tansey realized came from the dead Mollie. He swore softly under his breath.

Peter White said, 'I never like putting down an animal, but in this case there was no choice. Mrs Mariner will be very upset. She was fond of old Mollie.'

'Have you any idea what made her bolt?' asked Tansey. 'I gather she was a gentle beast.'

'The only thing that's occurred to me is that she might have been stung by a bee or a wasp. That's been known to happen.'

'What about a pellet from an air gun?' Tansey suggested and, when White stared at him, added, 'I'd like you to give her a good going-over to see if you can find any mark on her body – as soon as possible. Phone me at Kidlington. For the moment it's between us. Understand?'

'I'll do that.' White nodded. 'The insurance people will probably want it anyway.'

Having given Donaldson instructions that the ground

behind the hedges on either side of the road was to be fingertip searched for at least a hundred yards back from the scene of the accident, and any suspicious footprints or tyremarks photographed, Tansey turned his attention to Tom Richardson.

'Mr Richardson, you know who I am. Are you all right?' he inquired. 'Ought not you to have gone to hospital?'

'No. I didn't want to go. I'm OK – a bit shaken, but not hurt. It's that appalling smell.'

'Yes, let's go and sit in my car and you can tell me what happened.'

When they were seated, Richardson said, 'There's not much to tell. I'd been visiting an old client who wants to change her will and was driving back from Little Chipping. I was playing a tape or I might have heard the horse, but I didn't. I wasn't going fast. I only bought the Jag last month, and it is – or I suppose was – the apple of my eye. Now it's a wreck. It's amazing how much damage a horse can do.'

Tansey listened patiently, aware that the lawyer was more shaken than he cared to admit. He didn't try to hurry him. He was thankful that, considering the circumstances, the young man was so calm and sensible.

'But a car's only a car – even a Jag. It's Lady Rocque I should be thinking about,' Richardson went on. 'I'm probably going to have nightmares, but it must have been a terrifying experience for her. How she wasn't killed instantly, I don't know; it's a miracle she wasn't. She came galloping around the corner, obviously out of control. She was lying on the horse's neck, and her feet were out of the stirrups. Mind you, Chief Inspector, I didn't have much time to take this in. I braked automatically, but there was nothing else I could do. Lady Rocque seemed to slide off the horse sideways – that's what probably saved her – and the horse did its best to mount the Jag.'

'What did you do then?' Tansey prompted as Richardson stopped, breathing quickly.

'I got out of my car. I saw she was alive but unconscious, and probably badly hurt. I was scared of doing the wrong thing. I knew I mustn't move her. I covered her with a rug and used my mobile phone to call the police. Lord, I was thankful when they arrived. The horse was making pathetic little whinnying noises all the time. It – it was dreadful.'

Tansey nodded his understanding. 'I need to have a word with Sergeant Donaldson – incidentally, he'll cope with your car – then I'll be going to the hospital, so I'll drive you home or to your office, whichever you prefer, Mr Richardson. Perhaps you'd look in to the Colombury police station tomorrow and make an official statement.'

'Yes, of course, Chief Inspector.' Richardson shook his head as if to clear it. 'Many thanks.'

Tansey dropped Tom Richardson off at his office and drove to the hospital. He had no hope of being allowed to speak to Andrea Rocque, but he wanted to know how she was, and he was lucky enough to meet Dick Band, the police surgeon, in the entrance hall.

'Come along to the cafeteria, Tansey, and I'll buy you a coffee,' he said. 'You want to know about the Rocque woman, I presume.'

'You presume correctly,' Tansey said.

'Blessed by the gods! She could so easily have been killed or badly crippled, and all that beauty would have been lost. You've seen the scene of the accident – a hideous mess?'

'Yes. I arrived as White was shooting the poor horse.'

'M-mm! Nasty! Well, her ladyship escaped lightly. She's regained consciousness and she's being X-rayed, but it's clear she's not been desperately hurt. Concussion, I suspect, some cracked ribs and a broken bone or two. In fact, she had the devil's own luck.'

But for how long, Tansey wondered, would her luck last, before she *was* killed, or her husband, or Daphne Mariner. Although so far he had no proof he didn't believe that this latest incident had been a casual accident.

14

The unusual accident that had befallen Lady Rocque, wife of Sir Bertram Rocque, Bart., of Wychwood Manor, Oxon, the former actress Andrea Marston, not only made headlines the following day in the *Colombury Courier*, but was reported in the national press and mentioned on both radio and television newscasts. There were photographs of the beautiful Andrea in the tabloids and lurid pictures of what one enterprising reporter described as 'the fatal mare'.

This was more than enough to cause gifts of flowers and fruit to arrive at the hospital and inquiries to flood in, though by now it had been established, to Bertram's relief, that Andrea had suffered no more than three cracked ribs, a small broken bone in her ankle, some bruising and slight concussion. But there was also the matter of shock, and Andrea was happy to agree to Dr Band's suggestion that she should stay in hospital for two or three days.

When Chief Inspector Tansey arrived with permission to interview her, he found her propped up with pillows, her beauty enhanced by a bruised cheekbone. She was chatting on the phone to her friend, Marlene Sinclair, while Bertram sat beside her bed looking bored. Promising to ring back, she put down the receiver and gave Tansey her full attention.

'Chief Inspector, I'm sorry you're having to waste your time over my stupid accident.'

The dazzling smile which accompanied the remark made Tansey think he should say it was a pleasure, but he chose to be non-committal. 'I'm glad to see you're not badly hurt, Lady Rocque.'

'She could have been killed or horribly crippled,' Bertram

128

put in quickly, anxious that the seriousness of the situation should not be overlooked.

'Yes,' Tansey agreed. 'It was a wicked thing to do.'

'Wicked?' Andrea and Bertram spoke together.

Tansey looked from one to the other, but their expressions showed nothing but surprise. 'It's bad news, I regret to say. Someone who knew of Lady Rocque's riding lessons and approximately when she would be returning along that stretch of road, waited by the hedge and fired two pellets from an airgun into poor Mollie.'

'Oh no! No!' Andrea said, burying her face in her hands.

Bertram was on his feet instantly, putting his arms around her. 'Darling, don't cry! Please don't cry!'

Andrea pushed him away. 'How do you know this, Tansey?'

The chief inspector hesitated. He was not accustomed to being interrogated or to being called 'Tansey' in this manner, but the reason for Andrea Rocque's sudden lack of *savoir faire* was apparent. She was afraid, desperately afraid and she hadn't realized what she was saying. Nevertheless, the Rocques had to be told the truth.

Tansey said, 'I asked the vet, Peter White, to examine Mollie's carcass carefully. He phoned yesterday afternoon to tell me that he had found two pellets in the body – pellets of the kind that would have come from an air pistol or rifle. So there can be no doubt as to why the unfortunate horse bolted.'

'None of that was in the newspapers,' Andrea said accusingly.

She was appalled. The earlier incidents at the Manor, which had upset Bertram and Daphne so much, hadn't greatly affected her – except for the threatening telephone calls, and even these Christopher Portman had dismissed as not necessarily intended for her. But now she didn't care whether the attacks were personal or not. She was involved, the victim of one attack and a potential target for the next.

'It will be. The media will have to be informed, but I thought you should be told first,' Tansey said.

'Yes – yes. Good of you.' Bertram was visibly distressed.

'You should both take every precaution you can, sir,' Tansey warned. 'I'm on my way to Wychwood Manor and I intend to tell Mrs Mariner the same.'

'Every precaution!' Andrea scoffed. 'And what are you proposing to do except "make inquiries"? The bloody police are useless!'

Pointedly she turned her back on Tansey and half buried her face in the pillows. Bertram made a hopeless gesture, and opened his mouth as if to apologize for his wife, but Tansey waved the apology away and quietly let himself out of the room.

Chief Inspector Tansey arrived at Wychwood Manor simultaneously with Simon Wayne. They had spoken on the telephone but had not yet met. Unlike the previous day, it had started to rain earlier and the rain was now heavy.

'Even Daphne can't be working outside in this,' Wayne said. 'If she's not in the greenhouses, she'll be indoors.'

'In the office, gentlemen,' Alice informed them. 'You know the way, Mr Wayne.'

'Yes, indeed, Alice. Come along, Chief Inspector.'

He led Tansey through the Manor to the office at the far end of the house, giving him an opportunity to notice how run-down and in need of repair the whole place was. Daphne was just replacing the telephone receiver.

'Good morning,' she said. 'That was Bertram on the line.'

'And how is Andrea? I called the hospital earlier, but somehow hospitals never seem to give satisfactory answers,' Wayne said.

'She's not badly hurt. Some cracked ribs, a broken bone in her ankle – and shock, of course. She had an incredibly lucky escape. I can't believe anyone – Chief Inspector –' Daphne looked questioningly at Tansey.

'Mrs Mariner, I came to tell you about it – though I guess that Sir Bertram's already done that – and to warn you to take extra care of yourself, if that's at all possible.'

'Told her what?' Wayne asked, frowning. 'You both know something I don't.'

'Yes, Mr Wayne. Mollie, the mare, bolted because someone fired two airgun pellets into her.'

'Good heavens! But that's awful! And just when Bertram's decided to dispense with Crank's services. That's why I came over, Daphne, to get you to persuade him to have Crank and his dog back.'

Daphne shook her head. 'He won't. He sent Crank away yesterday evening because he was upset over what he believed was a chance accident to Andrea, and he never really liked having him around. But now he's learnt about the airgun attack, he'll convince himself that it was because the Manor was guarded and the man failed to poison the water supply, that he decided to attack Andrea.'

'Mrs Mariner, I think it's a pity about Crank,' Tansey said.

'A pity? Bloody foolish, I call it. Chris will not be pleased,' Wayne said.

'I'll make us some coffee.' Daphne got up to plug in the kettle and, her back turned, said, 'Have you been able to let Christopher know about Andrea, Simon?'

'Yes. He called last night from Paris and I told him. Of course, then I thought it was an accident. He's flying into Heathrow at noon today.'

'Good! He'll be able to see Andrea before she leaves.'

'Leaves? Hospital, you mean?'

'Yes, but she's not coming back here. Marlene Sinclair has invited her to join them in a villa the Sinclairs are renting in Spain, and she'll be going at the end of the week. Bertram's not over fond of the Sinclairs, but he's delighted that Andrea will be safely out of this madman's reach.'

'What about you, Daphne? Where are you going?'

'Don't be silly, Simon. I'm not Andrea. I couldn't possibly leave Bertram – or the business.'

'No. Stupid of me to think of it.' Wayne's smile was sardonic.

Tansey got up. 'Mrs Mariner, I must go. I won't have coffee, thank you. But I do reiterate, take care!'

'I will, Chief Inspector, I promise. Will you be able to find your way out?'

'Yes, don't bother.'

131

Wayne held up a restraining hand. 'Before you go, Chief Inspector, I have a message for you from Chris Portman. I was intending to get in touch. He knows you've been wanting to see him, and if it's convenient he'll be home any time after four today. Otherwise –'

'That will be fine,' Tansey said.

The difference between Wychwood Manor and Charlbury Hall was startling. The wrought iron gates, electronically controlled, the well-manicured grounds, the fine façade of the house and the white-coated manservant who opened the splendid mahogany front door to Chief Inspector Tansey at four-fifteen that afternoon all spoke of wealth. But Tansey had never been impressed by wealth, *per se*, whether inherited or self-generated; he was more interested in how those who possessed it used it, and as he was shown through a picture-lined hall, which ended in a wide stairway, and then to the right into a comparatively small sitting-room, he knew enough to realize that Christopher Portman, while appreciating what was beautiful, had done his best to avoid ostentation.

The sitting-room contained more pictures and several pieces of antique furniture, but there was a bookcase that overflowed on to the floor, a large television set and what Tansey knew was a sophisticated and expensive music centre. It was a pleasant, lived-in room. Tansey decided this was a room he would have enjoyed, except perhaps for the pictures.

He was standing in front of what looked to him like a collection of multi-coloured triangles when Portman came in, followed by Simon Wayne. Portman offered to shake hands, indicated a chair and said, 'I'm sorry we've not been able to meet before, Chief Inspector.'

'It's not important, sir,' Tansey said, and thought what an attractive man Christopher Portman was. 'May I assume that Mr Wayne has brought you up to date with the events at Wychwood Manor, and this last wicked attack on Lady Rocque?'

Portman nodded. 'Yes. It's very worrying. Are you getting anywhere with your inquiries?'

'There's not been much time,' Tansey said mildly. 'But I'm beginning to build up a preliminary picture of the character who is responsible.'

'Then you believe the incidents are all connected?'

'Yes, I don't think there's any doubt about that now.'

'Tell us what you know about this chap, Chief Inspector. We may be able to add a fact or two.'

'A picture of the chap? He's of medium height and build, according to Crank. Physically active. He's either a local or has been a local; he knows the district. He's free to go out at night without waking a wife or girlfriend, which suggests he's a loner. He's capable and efficient. He gets hold of whatever he needs for his nefarious acts. He probably rides a motorbike. He –'

They listened carefully to what he had to say, their expressions reflecting no more than interest, and Tansey was reminded that these were high-powered businessmen, not accustomed to betraying their emotions. But as he finished, admitting that he had no idea of the man's motive, he thought – it was more than an impression – that he saw a signal pass between them. It was as if Portman were querying something – some course of action – something to which Wayne assented.

'Chief Inspector,' Portman said at last. 'I think I should tell you about some dealings I had with a local man who rides a motorbike. It happened last year.'

'Last year?' Tansey was disappointed.

'Yes, last October, which makes it extremely difficult to believe that my experience can be relevant. However, the man in question was a nasty piece of work and it's just conceivable that he's surfaced again. So you should be told the facts. As you know, both Crank and Alice, the Manor housekeeper, believe the joker, as Bertram calls him, made off on a motorbike.'

Tansey was cautious. 'There are a lot of motorbikes around, sir, and October is almost ten months ago. Nevertheless, I should like to hear about your "experience", as you called it, and if there's any possibility of a connection I'll certainly check up on this man, whoever he is.'

'His name is Gavin Brail. He was a motor mechanic at the Windrush Garage in Colombury which, as you probably know, is owned and run by a chap called Field. Brail left at the end of last year in somewhat dubious circumstances and went to work in Bristol, but he's often back in Colombury because his wife's family lives there.' Portman hesitated. 'Chief Inspector, please understand I'm not accusing Brail, but I've come to the conclusion that this information should be available to you.'

'Yes, I understand,' said Tansey, who was wondering why Portman should be making such heavy weather of what was presumably a simple story.

'It was like this,' said Portman. 'One day last October, Lady Rocque telephoned me. She said she was bored, the others were busy, and would I like to take her out to lunch. She picked me up and we drove to Oxford, where we had a long protracted lunch. The intention was that she would drop me off at my house on her way back to the Manor, but she didn't feel well, so we went straight to the Manor and I brought the Toyota on back here, promising to have it returned the next day, which I did.'

'The Toyota?'

'Yes. That's the whole point. I was driving Sir Bertram's car when I was stopped by the police diverting the traffic because there had been a hit-and-run accident. A schoolboy from Coriston College had been knocked off his bicycle and killed, and the authorities had closed the road while they investigated. A motorcyclist drew up beside me, while the police officer was explaining all this, and heard the story. Subsequently he followed me until I got home, though there was nothing odd about this. We had both been directed to the same diversionary route.'

'You'd passed him on your way to the Manor,' Wayne reminded Portman.

'Oh yes. We had hooted at him because he was in the middle of the lane. Of course, I didn't realize it was the same man, and I thought no more about it until he tried to blackmail me, claiming he knew it was I who had earlier mown down that young – young –'

'Francis Carton.' Wayne supplied the name.

'He tried to blackmail you, Mr Portman? Why didn't you report the incident to the local police? Blackmail's a serious crime.'

'I probably should have done, but I had no proof. I didn't know who he was. I decided to take action myself.'

'I see,' said Tansey doubtfully. 'And why do you think he tried to blackmail *you*, not Sir Bertram?'

'I take it he saw me driving the Toyota and assumed I owned it.' Portman shrugged. 'Or maybe he thought I was a better source of money.'

'What happened next?' Tansey asked.

He was intrigued. Undoubtedly there was some truth in Portman's story. But the whole thing had been too smooth a concoction, too carefully rehearsed to be a completely acceptable version of events. Even Portman's hesitation over the boy's name, and Wayne's intervention, might well have been studied. Do they really expect me to believe all this? Tansey wondered.

'The rest is rather embarrassing,' Portman went on, 'but I've enough sense to know that once you pay a blackmailer you never get rid of him. So I arranged for two friends of mine from London to meet him, supposedly with the money – and they put the fear of God into him.'

'To such an extent that he got drunk and drove his motor-bike into a stone wall,' Wayne said. 'Luckily he wasn't hurt, and we've never heard from him since.'

'Then why on earth, after all these months, would he suddenly start this vendetta against Sir Bertram Rocque and Wychwood Manor?' Tansey asked.

'I know, I know,' Portman said. 'It would make more sense if he was attacking me, but we're pretty well guarded here at the Hall. The only explanation I can offer, if it is Brail – and the chances are it isn't – is that he believes that by harming the Rocques he is harming me. After all, they are close friends of mine. As for the time gap, I've no explanation for that.'

'Apart from the fact that he rides a motorbike and may want some kind of revenge for what he perhaps considers a wrong done to him, is there any other connection with –'

'He deserved all he got,' Wayne interjected. 'He wasn't physically hurt, and Chris paid his fine for driving under the influence and destroying property – the wall he crashed into.'

'Simon!'

'Well, it's true. And you had nothing to do with Field giving him the sack. He can't blame you for that.'

'Perhaps not, but – Chief Inspector, I paid the fine because I felt responsible for what had happened – a salve to my conscience, if you like – I certainly wasn't being noble and forgiving. Brail is a despicable character, but he has a wife and two boys, and in the circumstances I saw no reason why they should suffer more than necessary.'

'Very generous of you, sir, and I agree this Brail would appear to be a right villain, but I'm afraid he doesn't sound to me like the guilty party in the present case,' Tansey said. 'However, I'll make some inquiries, and in the meantime –'

'There is one other thing, Chief Inspector,' Portman interrupted. 'Anonymous phone calls – not to me, but to Lady Rocque. There are two that I know of, but there may have been more. They weren't personal, it appears. In each case, Lady Rocque just happened to be by the phone and pick it up.'

'What was said?'

'Approximately, "This is a warning. There's worse to come. You must pay for your sins". It really makes no sense, except as an attempt to frighten.'

'Neither Sir Bertram nor Mrs Mariner has ever mentioned any anonymous calls.' Tansey was doubtful.

'Lady Rocque may not have told them for fear of worrying them,' Portman said. 'Incidentally, Sir Bertram knows nothing about this Brail episode. None of them do.'

'I see,' said Tansey, who by now was far from sure what to believe and what to view with scepticism. 'As I said, sir, I'll certainly look into Mr Brail, but I don't hold out much hope that he's the man we're looking for – because of the lapse in time if nothing else.'

'I quite agree,' Portman said, 'but we thought it right you should be told about him. After all, it's essential the chap responsible should be found – now more than ever. After all, the earlier outrages were bad enough, horrible, frightening. But Lady Rocque could easily have been killed.'

'Yes, sir. I realize that,' Tansey said meekly.

But Chief Inspector Tansey was not feeling meek. On the contrary, he was angry. He felt that an attempt to manipulate him had been made and he disliked being manipulated, especially when he couldn't imagine why. His mind teemed with questions, for most of which he had no answers. Most importantly, why had Portman and Wayne produced this extraordinary and quite unnecessary story about Brail? There had to be a modicum of truth in it, for much of it could be checked – and indeed would have to be. But even if the whole tale were true, and Brail was seeking a late revenge it seemed unlikely he would have taken it out on Portman's 'close friends' – or had Portman really used 'close friends' as a euphemism for 'mistress'?

15

Thursday. It was Sergeant Donaldson's rest day, so he was not at the Colombury police station when Tansey arrived. Police Constable Wright was in charge. This turned out to be a piece of luck. Eager to ingratiate himself with a senior officer from Headquarters, Wright showed Tansey into Donaldson's office and quickly produced the file on the hit-and-run accident that had caused the death of Francis Carton, curbing his impatience until Tansey had studied it.

When the chief inspector returned the file, he ventured, 'I'm afraid there's not much to go on there, sir, but as you know there rarely is in such cases.'

'You didn't follow up the red paint found on the boy's bicycle?' Tansey said, thinking of the red Toyota he had seen the previous day in front of Wychwood Manor.

'No, sir. It wasn't possible without some other lead. We couldn't check all red vehicles in the district. I wish we could have done, though it might not have helped much. That wretched little boy! His death absolutely shattered his father. You can ask WPC Digby about that.'

'Why WPC Digby?'

'Sergeant Donaldson sent the two of us to break the news to Mr Carton, sir. There isn't a Mrs Carton. It was dreadful. The poor man broke down and wept. Then he became angry and cursed the driver who was responsible for his son's death.'

'Cursed him, did he? There's nothing about that in the report of the interview.'

'No, sir. Sergeant Donaldson didn't think it relevant. "Hysteria," he said. But Mr Carton did say something like,

"I'll kill the bugger if you ever find him". We were thankful when his friend Mr Hauler arrived. Mr Hauler was one of Frankie's schoolmasters at Coriston.'

'I see,' said Tansey. 'That's very interesting, Wright.'

'Yes, sir.'

It was interesting, Tansey reflected. Here was a direct threat, albeit from a man in great distress, against the driver of the vehicle that had killed his son. According to Christopher Portman, Gavin Brail had believed the vehicle was the red Toyota belonging to Bertram Rocque, but the driver had been Portman.

Edmund Carton might have gathered a different version of the event. If he thought that Sir Bertram was responsible for Frankie's death, he had an excellent motive for the persecution of the Rocques. But, once again the question arose: why the delay of so many months?

'Incidentally, while I'm here, I'd like to look into another accident, though not a very serious one. A chap called Gavin Brail, who used to be a mechanic at Field's garage, got drunk last autumn and drove into a wall. Does that ring a bell with you, Wright?'

The young constable stared at him, frowning. 'Yes, sir. I knew Brail when he was at Field's. We used to meet quite often in the pub – the Windrush Arms.'

'He does drink, then?'

'No more than I do, sir.' Wright was reproachful. 'In fact, I was extremely surprised about his accident, the more because to my knowledge he never touched spirits – and the evidence suggested he'd been on gin. I thought maybe some of his pals might have played a trick on him but, if that was the truth, he never let on.'

'Was his blood tested?'

'No, sir. The evidence was overwhelming. As I say, he stank of gin and was semi-conscious when the vicar from Little Chipping found him, and he was carted off to hospital. There was some trouble about us not having tested him, and the magistrate said that in the absence of such evidence, he wouldn't take away his licence, but merely fine him.'

'Was he badly hurt?'

'Not a bit. He told Rita, his wife, that he didn't even have a hangover the next day. A funny business, it was. But some kind of benefactor paid his fine and he didn't do too badly. He lives in Bristol now.'

Thanking Wright, Tansey departed from the police station. He had learnt more from ten minutes' chat with the constable than from reading innumerable papers. And, except in the unlikely event of a confession by Gavin Brail, he had received as much confirmation of Portman's story as he could expect. He wished it were possible to check it all.

Next, Tansey drove out to Coriston College. He was far from sure what he expected to learn there, but it seemed that Portman had wanted him to inquire into Frankie Carton's death, and his talk with PC Wright had encouraged him to feel curious about it.

This was not the chief inspector's first visit to the College. Not too long ago he had investigated the murder of one of its students. But there was a new headmaster now, younger, more efficient, eager to improve the image of the school, which over the years had had its ups and downs, but had grown from a small snobbish boarding establishment to include day students and greatly improve its academic status, though its fees remained high and out of reach of the average income.

Tansey had telephoned ahead, and Gordon Stanton, the headmaster, was expecting him, so he was shown at once into his study. Stanton, a tall, thin man with a beaked nose who in his gown looked like a giant bird, rose to his feet and offered Tansey his hand.

'Good morning, Chief Inspector. Please sit down and tell me how I can help you.' Stanton had a nasal voice and a pleasantly relaxed manner.

'I'm interested in a former pupil of yours, sir, a Francis Carton, who was killed last year in a hit-and-run accident.'

'May I ask why, Chief Inspector? I gathered the police had given up hope of finding the culprit long ago.'

'It's come up in connection with another case, sir.'

'I see.' Stanton formed his hands into a pyramid, which

he studied for a minute in silence. Then he said, 'I hope this is unlikely to prove detrimental to Coriston's reputation, Chief Inspector.'

Tansey was surprised. 'I should think it most unlikely, sir.'

Stanton nodded his acceptance of the chief inspector's assurance. 'All right. Francis Carton was fourteen when he was killed. He had been at Coriston for two years. A scholarship boy. Clever. Should have gone on to a major university. His home life was rather sad. His mother was dead, and he lived with his father in a small house on the other side of Colombury. Edmund Carton is a freelance journalist, not too successful, and I suspect that money was pretty tight.'

'What about friends, relations?'

'No close friends. I believe there was an aunt who lived in Scotland.'

'You say no close friends, sir. I understand that Mr Hauler, one of your staff, was friendly with the family.'

Stanton's mouth twisted in a sardonic smile. 'Ah, now you've come to the point, Chief Inspector.'

Tansey, who had no idea what the headmaster meant, was tempted to say, 'Have I?' or 'What point?' He had been thinking that he was wasting his time at Coriston and had mentioned Hauler's name merely out of politeness, to show an interest that he didn't feel in what Stanton was saying. But he managed to stay silent.

'Chief Inspector, I must correct you.' Stanton sighed. 'Jocelyn Hauler is no longer a member of the staff here. He was on a contract and we did not renew it. It was a mutual arrangement. Both Hauler and I agreed that he was not suited to being a schoolmaster.'

'Why? Was he a poor teacher?'

'No, Chief Inspector. Let us come clean with each other, as they say. You tell me why you're interested in Hauler, and I'll tell you why we let him go. You must understand it's my duty to safeguard the reputation of Coriston, and if Hauler is in any trouble –'

Dick Tansey was an experienced police officer, but the conversation had been so obscure that only now did he grasp what Stanton was saying, or rather not saying. The man's reticence and the suggestion of some sort of bargain over an exchange of information in what was, after all, an official inquiry annoyed him, but he realized that he would gain by cooperating.

'Mr Hauler is not in any trouble, sir, and Coriston is not involved. But I do wish to know about Hauler's relationship with Frankie Carton. He was fond of the boy?'

'Too fond. Oh, I'm not suggesting there was ever any actual impropriety, either with Francis or any of the other students, but a schoolmaster has to be careful not to show favouritism or to – to let his feelings get the better of him. Hauler was inordinately upset over young Carton's death, and attached himself to the father until Carton senior left Colombury. It caused talk, a certain amount of sniggering among the older boys. From the point of view of the school, the situation was altogether undesirable.'

'Thank you, sir. Thank you for being so frank. I'm most grateful,' Tansey said truthfully; he had learnt more than he had hoped for. 'I suppose you wouldn't have Mr Carton's address. You said he had left Colombury.'

'My secretary will get it for you.'

And, from the headmaster's secretary in the outer office, Tansey acquired not only the address and phone number of Edmund Carton, who was said to be living with his sister in Scotland, but also the address of Jocelyn Hauler, who was at present working in an antiquarian bookshop in Abingdon.

Next stop Abingdon, Tansey thought, but on leaving Coriston College he felt overwhelmed by fatigue, a reminder of the weeks he had spent in hospital and he drove at a steady pace back to Kidlington. He knew that he could have gone home; no one would have minded. But he hated to give in. At least in the office he could go through his files and consider his next move in the Rocque case. Besides, his unexpected appearance before lunch could easily shock Hilary.

One of the WPCs brought him sandwiches and coffee from the canteen, and he settled down for an afternoon of paper-work, though he found it difficult to concentrate. He kept on thinking about Portman and Wayne and the act they had put on for his benefit. Their story of the attempted blackmail by the garage mechanic had been partially checked; it was a pity Brail now lived in Bristol and wasn't readily available. He wondered how often he came to Colombury.

As his thoughts drifted from one subject to the next, Tansey remembered that he had not asked Daphne Mariner if, like her sister-in-law, she had received any anonymous phone calls, and he was stretching out his hand for the phone when it burred.

'Sir, I have a Mrs Daphne Mariner on the line. Will you take her call?'

'Yes, indeed. Put it through.'

Tansey waited uneasily for Mrs Mariner to speak. He could think of only one reason why she should have telephoned him. Something else had happened. There had been another attack on the Rocques? More damage done to their property? To her? To Sir Bertram? Lady Rocque was still in hospital –

'Chief Inspector Tansey?' Her voice was not quite steady, and he feared the worst.

'Yes, Mrs Mariner. Are you all right?'

'Fine, thank you. A little shaken, perhaps. I've had a most extraordinary experience. Don't laugh! I know it sounds absurd, but I've been assaulted in Silverman's – that's the biggest supermarket in Colombury.'

'What? Are you hurt?'

'No, not really. A few minor cuts and bruises and, as I said, a bit shaken.'

'What happened?'

'I had some shopping to do, so I made myself respectable and drove into Colombury. I thought I could do the shopping, say hello to Andrea and bring Bertram home. Jimmy, who drives our van, had taken him in earlier. Silverman's was almost empty. I was standing in front of some shelves of tinned soups when one of those metal trolleys was rammed into my back. I grabbed the shelves and the whole lot, tins and all, came down on top of me.'

'Oh dear!' Tansey was sympathetic. 'Mrs Mariner, I hate to ask you this, but could it possibly have been an accident

– an accident after which the person responsible panicked and didn't stop to say how sorry they were?'

'No! Definitely not, Chief Inspector. It was done with considerable force and I'm sure it must have been deliberate. One moment I was alone in what is quite a small aisle, and the next I was being bombarded with cans of soup. They were heavy. So were the shelves – Silverman's is an old-fashioned place in many ways and they were made of heavy wood. Oh, there was no question of my being killed, but I could have broken an arm or a leg or suffered a head injury. At the very least it was intimidatory.'

'Someone came to your help?'

'Yes, indeed. The staff and a couple of other shoppers heard the noise and came running. Everyone was most kind. But they assumed it was an accident and – I know you won't approve – I couldn't face the explanations and complications if I claimed that someone had attacked me. The manager would have insisted on sending for a doctor and the police, in case I sued the place for damages or anything, and all I wanted to do was collect Bertram and get home. So I blamed myself for a mishap. Sorry, Chief Inspector.'

'I understand, Mrs Mariner. Who knew you were going to the supermarket?'

'No one – not even Alice. I just decided on the spur of the moment, so it can't have been a premeditated attack.'

'Then it must have been chance, or you were recognized in Colombury and followed.'

'That's exactly what worries me. It's not a pleasant idea. It means I should be constantly looking over my shoulder.'

'Until we find this crazy character, yes.'

'Do you believe he's crazy?'

'To be candid, no, I do not. There's some purpose behind what he does. Mrs Mariner, what time did this happen to you?'

'About one-thirty. I couldn't phone till I got home. Why?'

Tansey didn't answer her question. Instead, he said, 'There's something I wanted to ask you earlier. Have you had any anonymous or curious phone calls lately?'

'Funny phone calls?' She took a moment to think. 'You don't mean wrong numbers. Obscene calls?'

'No – more like threatening calls.'

'No-o, though there was one odd call last week. I thought at the time it must have been a Jehovah's Witness or a member of some such outfit. It didn't exactly tell me that the Kingdom of Heaven was nigh. It was more or less a demand for me to repent of my sins – or I'd be sorry.'

Much the same message as Lady Rocque was said to have received, Tansey thought. 'Did it scare you, Mrs Mariner?'

'No. I just banged down the receiver. I was busy and couldn't be bothered. I'd forgotten all about it until your question. Are you suggesting it might have been from our – our enemy, if that's the right word, Chief Inspector?'

'I was wondering,' Tansey admitted.

He continued to wonder after he had said goodbye to Daphne Mariner. He wondered if the difference between Daphne Mariner's reaction and that of Andrea Rocque was due to the characters of the women, or if Mrs Mariner had a clear conscience and Lady Rocque did not. But it seemed unprofitable to pursue the idea.

There were more important things to worry about. The boldness and the opportunism of the attack on Daphne Mariner in the supermarket so soon after the one on Andrea Rocque was extremely worrying. Clearly, the attacks had not ended, and indeed, since he was sure that the news of his own involvement in the case had spread, this last one seemed to him almost a personal challenge. He might not have wanted the job, he thought grimly, but he was definitely going to see it through now.

16

When Tansey arrived at his office on Friday morning slightly later than usual, his phone was burring angrily.

'Hello! Tansey here.'

It was the duty officer. 'Chief Inspector,' he said, 'a PC Wright from Colombury has been trying to contact you. He says that a man called Brail is visiting his in-laws at the moment, and perhaps you'd be interested in talking to him. I hope that makes sense, sir.'

'It does indeed. Many thanks. Get on to Colombury for me and arrange for PC Wright to lay on a meeting with him at the station there as soon as possible.'

Postponing the trip to Abingdon he had planned for that morning to see Jocelyn Hauler, Tansey set off for Colombury. He decided on a tactful approach to Gavin Brail, and if possible to avoid mentioning the attempt at blackmail.

Wright was on the phone when the chief inspector walked into the station. 'Like half an hour ago,' he was saying cheerfully. 'This way you don't have to offer the family any explanations. And not to worry, Gavin. We've nothing against you. We just need your help.'

He listened for a moment, said, 'Fine,' and put down the receiver and turned to Tansey. 'As I told you, sir, I know Gavin Brail quite well. So I hope I was taking the right line.'

'Yes, indeed,' said Tansey. 'Clever of you to let me know he was here. Will he be long?'

'A short while, I guess, sir. He's only staying around the corner.'

Brail arrived within ten minutes, initially full of bluster. 'What's all this about then?' he demanded. 'A chief inspec-

146

tor? Must be important.' Tansey heard him from the inner office, and reflected that aggressiveness often concealed a bad conscience.

Once in an interview room, however, sitting across a desk from Tansey, Brail's attitude changed perceptibly. 'What am I supposed to have done, sir?' he asked with an ingratiating smile.

'Not you, Mr Brail, I hope. Other people,' said Tansey reassuringly. 'You live in Bristol now, I gather — a fair distance from Colombury — but you still keep your ties here.'

'My wife's mum and dad live here, and some of the rest of the family.'

'So you're in touch. You must know about the persecution that the people at Wychwood Manor have been suffering, the destruction of property, the vandalism — and recently this personal attack on Lady Rocque.'

'I've heard about them, yes.' Brail was wary.

'Mr Brail, what I have to say now is in confidence. There's reason to believe that these incidents are connected with the hit-and-run accident that caused the death of young Francis Carton last autumn. What I want you to do is to be good enough to tell me all you can about that accident.'

Gavin Brail gobbled. Tansey saw his Adam's apple bob up and down. The chief inspector had spoken with an air of complete certainty that was not justified and, as Brail struggled to produce an articulate answer, he looked him in the eye and smiled confidently. He wished he could have known what was passing through Brail's mind.

'What — what makes you think I know anything at all about that — that accident?' Brail stammered eventually.

'Oh, come, let's not go into that, Mr Brail. I take it that you're not personally responsible for these incidents, which have become more and more serious, and certainly warrant a prison sentence.'

'No, I'm not responsible for them, and I can prove it! I live in Bristol. I don't know what dates these things took place, but I must have an alibi for some of them. Yes, Lady Rocque and her horse.' Brail was babbling. 'I was in the garage that day. I remember when Rita, my wife, told me about it —'

'All right. Calm down, Mr Brail. Tell me about Francis Carton's accident,' Tansey said, and, when Brail had given his version, he added, 'You know, do you, that the red Toyota that you believe killed the boy was the same car that Mr Portman had borrowed from Sir Bertram Rocque, and that you saw him driving later alone?'

It was a trick question, and Brail fell into the trap.

'If you mean can I prove it, no,' he said, 'but if it wasn't, why didn't he –'

'Why didn't he appeal to the police when you accused him? Better not go into that, perhaps. Some powerful men prefer to take matters into their own hands, and it's not a good idea to trifle with them, as I'm sure you'll agree.'

Brail glared at him, but didn't speak. It was obvious to him that, while Tansey might not know the whole story, he knew enough to make life difficult should he choose to do so. It didn't take Brail long to realize that his best bet would be to cooperate. So, when the chief inspector asked him whom he had told about his suspicions of the Toyota, he unhesitatingly named Edmund Carton.

'I wrote him a letter,' he said. 'I thought he had a right to know. After all, he was the boy's father.'

'When was this?'

'End of January, after I'd gone to live in Bristol. More than six months ago.'

'Did Edmund Carton get in touch with you?'

'No.' Brail hesitated. 'I didn't sign the letter.'

Tansey nodded. A six months' delay before seeking revenge was more plausible than nine months', but only just. Nevertheless, Edmund Carton had the best possible motive.

'Can you remember what you wrote in this letter, Mr Brail?'

'What I told you, that I'd seen this car – the one what must have killed the boy, that it belonged to Sir Bertram Rocque, but later I saw Mr Portman driving it. Anyway, Chief Inspector, Carton took no action that I know of. Perhaps he never got the letter.'

'Perhaps. You sent it to his Colombury address?'

'Yes, he was still here then.'

'Did you tell anyone else of your suspicions?'

'No, Chief Inspector. Of course, Mr Portman knew,' Brail said doubtfully.

Tansey gave him a long searching look, not bothering to hide his contempt, but decided not to refer to the blackmail attempt again. 'Right!' He stood up. 'That's all for the present. We know where to find you if it becomes necessary. Meanwhile, Mr Brail, you are not to mention the conversation we've had this morning to anyone. To anyone. Do you understand?'

'Yes, sir.'

Simon Wayne had been right, Tansey thought, as he showed a chastened Brail out of the interview room. The man had deserved what he got.

After an early lunch at the Windrush Arms, Chief Inspector Tansey started for Abingdon and, he hoped, a meeting with Jocelyn Hauler, Francis Carton's former schoolmaster, but on a whim he decided to go out of his way to take a look at the house where Frankie had lived with his father.

The house was up a lane, a small characterless building, but not neglected. The paintwork was in good condition, the plot of grass in front was neatly mown, and the strip of flowerbed that edged it was clear of weeds. The upstairs windows were half open, as if to air the rooms. Someone was taking care of the place.

For half a minute, Tansey expected the front door to open, and to find himself confronted by Edmund Carton, but no one appeared. He got out of his car. He rang the doorbell without result. And he walked slowly around the house, peering in the windows. There were obvious signs of habitation, flowers in the sitting-room, a newspaper and a magazine lying on a table, fresh vegetables in the kitchen. Was Edmund Carton back in Colombury? Tansey wondered. The impression he had received from everyone to whom he had spoken of Carton was that he was living with his sister in Scotland, but –

Tansey turned his car and set off down the lane. This time he was absolutely determined to let nothing distract him from going to Abingdon. After all, according to the head-master of Coriston, Jocelyn Hauler could be said to have a motive, not dissimilar from Edmund Carton's, for avenging Frankie's death; he too had apparently loved the boy.

Tansey found Hauler in the antiquarian's shop opposite the town church, carefully dusting a row of beautifully bound books. He was alone; the owner was out and there were no customers. Having introduced himself, Tansey immediately mentioned that he had been at Coriston College the previous day, and he saw Hauler stiffen at the name of the school.

'So what do you want?' he demanded abruptly.

'The answers to just a few questions,' Tansey said for the umpteenth time in his career. 'Some of them may seem unusual, Mr Hauler, but please bear with me. First, do you know who I mean by the Rocques of Wychwood Manor near Colombury?'

Hauler frowned. 'I know of them. I read about Lady Roc-que's horse bolting and immolating itself on a car. But I've never met any of them. What have they got to do with Coriston?' He was clearly puzzled.

Tansey said, 'It's been suggested that a car they own, or one similar to it, was responsible for the death of Francis Carton.'

'Dear God!' Hauler said, with sudden emotion. 'So it wasn't a piece of nastiness after all,' he added, almost to himself.

Automatically, he picked up a book and started dusting it, as if the chief inspector had not been there. Tansey waited.

Suddenly Hauler burst out, 'I hate anonymous letters. I've good reason to. But you've been to Coriston, Chief Inspector, talked to the headmaster. You can guess. It's amazing how cruel people can be, especially young people. You'd have thought that when someone had died, been killed tragically – ' His voice broke. 'But that wasn't what I was talking about.'

'What were you talking about, Mr Hauler?'

'One particular anonymous letter, that my friend, Edmund Carton, received. It said the writer knew that Frankie had been killed by a red Toyota belonging to Sir Bertram Rocque

150

of Wychwood Manor, but that his friend, Christopher Portman, not Sir Bertram, had probably been the driver.'

'You saw this letter? You read it?'

'No. Edmund had burnt it, but he told me what it contained and we discussed what, if any, action he should take – and we decided the letter should be ignored because it didn't offer any proof and there was probably no truth in it anyway.'

Tansey didn't query the veracity of what Hauler had told him. Instead, he wondered aloud why Carton had burnt the letter before showing it to Hauler.

'This was last January, and his sister was staying with him at the time. She was helping him pack up. He was going to live with her in Scotland. Poor Edmund! He wasn't looking forward to the arrangement. His sister's very possessive and much too curious. Which is why, when she wanted to read the letter, he just said it was from some crank claiming he knew who had killed Frankie, and chucked it on the fire.'

Tansey nodded his understanding; Hauler's account agreed with what Gavin Brail had said. 'When did you last see Mr Carton?' he asked.

'In January. That was the last time.'

'The house is occupied at present. Would he have returned to Colombury without telling you?'

'Oh no! Definitely not. Those will be his tenants there. He's letting the place. His sister wanted him to sell and move in with her for good, but he wouldn't commit himself. He wasn't really happy living with her. I had a letter from him at Easter, and he sounded horribly depressed. I've not heard from him since.'

Tansey murmured sympathy and stood up from the stool on which he had been perched. 'I think that's all, Mr Hauler. Thank you for your help.'

Clutching a couple of books, so that there was no possibility of shaking hands, Hauler followed Tansey to the door of the shop. 'I hope you find whoever killed Frankie, Chief Inspector,' he said, but almost as if it were an afterthought.

Tansey had a fair idea who this might be, but for the moment he intended to keep his thoughts to himself. He had no proof, and he doubted if he would find any. Moreover, Francis Carton's death was outside his remit, unless he could prove that it was relevant to the persecution of Bertram Rocque and his family.

'By the way, Mr Hauler,' he said at the door. 'I meant to ask you. Do you ride a motorbike?'

'No. I have a car. A Renault.' Hauler looked slightly embarrassed. 'I – I have a private income, thanks to my parents. I'm not dependent on my work.'

'You're lucky,' Tansey said lightly.

But on the way back to Headquarters he speculated about Jocelyn Hauler – and Edmund Carton. They each had a motive for persecuting the Rocques, or could believe they had; they were friends and might have collaborated in a common cause; Carton's time was his own, and Hauler had admitted to financial resources; they had lived in the district and would know it well.

They were certainly both potential suspects, together or separately but, taken separately, Edmund Carton seemed to Tansey the more likely culprit. He had been devoted to his son, surely a closer relationship than that of presumably unrequited love for a pupil. He had threatened to kill the individual responsible for the boy's death. He was an unhappy man, whose only relative appeared to be a possessive sister.

However, what was in Carton's favour, if it could be shown to be true, and would indeed quash all possibility of his guilt, was his continuous domicile in Scotland since the New Year. On the other hand, if for some reason he had been unable to get away from his sister until the last few weeks when the attacks on the Rocques had taken place, the time gap between the receipt of Brail's letter in January and these attacks could be explained, and one nagging problem would be resolved. But it didn't explain why no attempt had been made to attack Christopher Portman and *his* household – unless this was still to come.

As soon as he reached Headquarters, Tansey telephoned the house in Peebles where Edmund Carton was supposed to be living with his sister. There was no answer. He tried again before he left for home, with the same result. He made two more attempts, the first at nine o'clock that evening from his home, and the second at eight the following morning. There was still no answer.

And Hilary revolted. 'Dick, it's Saturday! You're not a member of the Serious Crime Squad at present. You're not even meant to be on full-time duty. You shouldn't be working at the weekend. Forget it. These people are just away for a few days – a long weekend, Thursday to Tuesday. Take my advice and leave it until next week.'

It was advice he was to regret taking, but he never admitted this to his wife.

17

On Saturday, the Sinclairs collected Lady Rocque from the hospital in their Rolls Royce. She had refused absolutely to return to Wychwood Manor before going to Spain. She had made a list of clothes and belongings that she wanted to take with her; Daphne had packed a couple of bags and Bertram had delivered them to the hospital. Andrea had also extracted a sizeable sum in traveller's cheques from Bertram in order to supplement her 'miserable garments' in the excellent shops which Marlene had assured her existed in the south. That it was money intended for the insurance premium due on the Manor, she neither knew nor cared. Daphne, who would have cared and would have said so forcibly, was not told of the arrangement. That inevitably she would find out was one of Bertram's many worries.

On the Monday after Andrea had departed with the Sinclairs, he set off for Oxford and a call on his bank manager. He was not in the best of moods. He already missed his wife, the more so because he was unhappy about her; he didn't like the brash Marlene Sinclair or such friends of hers as he had met, and he resented Andrea being beholden to them for a holiday, which he couldn't afford to give her himself.

All his worries, it seemed to him, centred around money or the lack of it. He desperately needed a larger overdraft if he were to meet the bills that would come in at the end of the month, many of them stamped with the ominous words 'Final Demand', and some, such as the electricity, threatening the immediate withdrawal of service. He had never been in so deep a hole before, but there had been many unexpected expenses recently, mostly thanks to the fact that he was

154

being persecuted by this unknown character. At least he wouldn't have to explain that to his bank manager as it was public knowledge; he hoped the situation would make the man sympathetic.

Bertram reached the place where Mollie had bolted, and was reminded of the last attack, which could have resulted in Andrea's death. It was an appalling thought. Suddenly he decided that he was glad she was safe in Spain. He didn't care how much she spent or what she did. Providing that she came back to him –

He had not been driving fast. There was a certain amount of tourist traffic, cars, bicycles, hikers, at this time of year and, though there were not a great many, they tended to usurp the crown of the narrow roads. Possibly the thought of them caused him to drive a shade more carefully than usual, and this may have saved him from a crippling accident.

As he rounded a corner, he accelerated slightly on seeing a straight stretch of empty road ahead. Suddenly there was a dull thud and a black haze spread over the windscreen. Unable to see, he braked sharply. If he had been driving faster he might have hit the bank at the side of the lane with considerable force. As it was, the car merely mounted the narrow verge, its front wheels skidding into the ditch, so that it came to rest with little more than a very hard bump against a tree.

It was bad luck that Bertram should have been hurt at all. Indeed, it was not until he stretched out his hand to open the car door and get out, that he realized he was a casualty. Then a searing pain went through his arm and for a moment he lost consciousness.

'Are you all right?' An anxious face had appeared at the car window.

Bertram did his best to smile at the elderly man standing beside the Toyota, but what emerged was a grimace rather than a smile. 'I'm afraid not,' he said. 'Perhaps you would help. First, would you reach in and turn off the ignition. Then if you'd open the car door and undo my seat belt, I'll see if I can get out.'

'Are you sure you should?'

'No, but I can't stay here. Do you by any chance have a phone in your car?'

The man shook his head. 'Wait a minute. There's something else coming. Sounds like a car. At least he can go for help.'

In the event that was not necessary. As luck would have it, the newcomer was a police officer with a radio phone. He spoke to his station in Colombury, briefly explained the situation and asked for assistance and an ambulance.

'Sir, I think it best if you don't try to move until the ambulance arrives,' he said to Bertram, who had been gingerly testing his limbs and had decided that only his right shoulder and arm were hurt. 'It won't be long. We'll get you to the hospital in no time.'

'Oh God!' Bertram groaned aloud, not from pain, but at the thought that this was yet one more disaster that had befallen them.

As soon as he reached his office, Chief Inspector Tansey had tried the Peebles number of Mrs Randelson, Edmund Carton's sister, in the hope that, if they had been away for the weekend, they might have returned home on Sunday evening, but there was still no reply. As Carton was unavailable, he decided to try to eliminate some of the other possible, if not probable, suspects.

He started with the least likely, Gavin Brail. Having obtained from Field, the owner of the Windrush Garage, the name of Brail's place of employment in Bristol, he phoned and asked to speak to the manager. When he had been put through, he explained he was making inquiries about a serious road accident that had occurred on a certain date – he gave the date on which Andrea Rocque's old mare had bolted into the path of a Jaguar – and said it was believed that Mr Brail, at present a mechanic in Bristol, had been a witness.

The manager thought for a moment. Then, 'He's not here today,' came the reply Tansey had expected. 'I'm afraid he's not due back until Tuesday. He has a long weekend off.'

'But perhaps you could help me yourself. Could you check to see if Mr Brail was working in your garage that day? The identification could have been an error, in which case –'

'Sure. Hang on, Chief Inspector.'

While he waited Tansey could hear voices and the various distinctive sounds associated with a large and apparently flourishing garage. Brail was a relative newcomer there, and it was unlikely that the manager would be prepared to lie on his behalf. Tansey was confident he would be able to trust the answer.

'Chief Inspector?' There was a muted laugh on the line. 'Afraid you've got the wrong man. According to our time sheets, Brail was right here the whole of the day you mentioned and, in fact, worked overtime.'

'Thanks a lot,' said Tansey. 'I'm most grateful. I thought it might well be an error, but it's nice to have confirmation.'

One gone, Tansey thought, and tried the estate agents where David Garson now worked. Here luck was with him once again; Garson was out of the office. He repeated the story he had told the manager of the Bristol garage, but this time a response was slow to come. Eventually it emerged that Garson was said to have been showing a property in Burford to a prospective client the morning of the supposed road accident into which Tansey was inquiring.

'And he was in Burford all the morning?' Tansey said, disappointed.

'Yes. It was a large property, and the client was late arriving. But wait a minute, Chief Inspector. Here's our Mr Oswald, who's learning the business. He was with Mr Garson that day. Would you like to speak to him?'

'Please,' said Tansey at once.

His luck held. Garson too could be eliminated. Oswald confirmed that he had been in David Garson's company all the relevant morning. They hadn't been near Colombury, and had seen no accident.

Tansey agreed that there must have been a mistake, as he had thought. He thanked Oswald, apologized for taking up his time and said goodbye. He was considering Jocelyn Hauler when his own phone buzzed.

Sergeant Donaldson was on the line. 'I thought you should be told at once, sir, as it's your case now. Sir Bertram Rocque has had an accident – fortunately not serious, but they're giving him a check-up at the hospital.'

'What sort of accident?'

'He appears to have driven into a tree.'

'Any witnesses?'

'To the event – no, sir.'

Tansey thought that Donaldson sounded smug, but he couldn't blame him; the big man from Headquarters was doing no better than the local police in finding the character who was persecuting the Rocques.

'Right, Sergeant. I'll be along.'

When Tansey arrived at the hospital and inquired for Sir Bertram Rocque, he was asked to wait as the patient was still in X-ray. Resenting the waste of time, he sat down. Immediately, an elderly grey-haired man came and sat opposite him.

'Excuse me, Chief Inspector,' he said, 'but I couldn't help overhearing. I myself am waiting to discover how Sir Bertram is. You see, I feel vaguely responsible. I'm Bernard Osterly, a retired civil servant. I live with my wife outside Little Chipping.'

'You didn't witness the accident, Mr Osterly?'

'No, I didn't, but I gathered from Sir Bertram – he was perfectly conscious, you know – that as he came around a corner his windscreen suddenly went blank, and he drove off the road. The police officer who came on us next and was able to send for help on his radio telephone thought Sir Bertram might have had a blackout, because the windscreen wasn't crazed or shattered, but Sir Bertram denied this.'

'So it can't have been a large stone then,' Tansey said, half to himself.

'Personally I think it was some sort of earthball,' Bernard Osterly volunteered. 'Like a snowball, but made of earth. It would break up on impact, spread ground over the glass and cause a driver to lose control. Then, if the earth were dry, the collision would jerk most of it away. There were bits of grass and soil on the bonnet of the Toyota. I pointed them out to the policeman, but I don't think he believed my theory.

However, something very similar happened to a friend of mine once. It was some youths larking about. My friend was lucky and wasn't hurt, but it could cause a serious accident – like now.'

'Did you see any youths larking about in the vicinity today, sir?'

'No, Chief Inspector, I didn't. Nevertheless, there's the evidence of the grass and soil on the bonnet.'

'Did you see anyone who might conceivably have thrown this earthball?' Tansey was more impressed by Osterly's suggestion than the police officer had been, but then he had reason to be, since Bertram Rocque was the accident victim.

'No, I must admit I didn't. I noticed a family on bicycles wobbling along, mother and father and two children – you have to be so careful to avoid people like that – and a car. Oh, and a young man on a motorcycle who startled me by suddenly riding very fast out of one of those field entrances shortly before I found poor Sir Bertram.'

The motorbike again, Tansey thought, and said, 'How do you know he was a young man, sir?'

Mr Osterly gave Tansey a curious look. 'I stand corrected, Chief Inspector. I don't know. I got the impression that he was younger than I am by the way he rode his bike – certainly more athletically than I could have done – but it was only an impression. He had on a crash helmet – black, it was – that completely hid his face. Come to think of it, for all I saw, it could have been a woman.'

A nurse interrupted them to say that Sir Bertram had no broken bones, and refused to stay in overnight. His sister was going to take him home. If the chief inspector would like to talk to him while he was waiting for some painkilling capsules to be brought – She looked doubtfully at Mr Osterly.

Osterly took the hint. 'I'll be off then,' he said. 'With you and his sister, Chief Inspector, he'll be in good hands. Incidentally, you know where to find me, if you should want to. I'm sure it was an earthball.'

'An earthball?' the nurse queried as she led Tansey along a corridor and pointed to a room at the end.

'Just something we were discussing,' Tansey said lightly.

He reached the room that the nurse had indicated. The door was ajar and, as he hesitated whether to knock or walk straight in, he heard Bertram's voice. Sir Bertram was angry.

'No, Daphne! Definitely not. The poor girl's only just got to Spain. She hasn't had time to relax and start to enjoy herself.'

'Why should she enjoy herself when –'

'Don't be selfish, Daphne. Andrea had a dreadful experience. She could easily have been killed, as I keep telling you. As it was, she was badly hurt and very frightened. All I've done is drive into a ditch. I've not even broken my shoulder, though I must say it felt like it when I first tried to move.'

'Bertram, you may not have broken any bones, but you've wrenched your shoulder and you're having a lot of discomfort. You're going to be incapacitated for at least a week. Andrea could be a big help. She could drive you into the hospital for this physiotherapy you've got to have –'

'No, Daphne! I don't intend to argue. I don't want Andrea to come home. I'll cope.'

'I hope I shall!'

Suddenly conscious that he was eavesdropping and that a nurse was approaching along the corridor, Tansey knocked loudly on the door. There was instant silence and he walked into the room. But any embarrassment was prevented by the arrival of the nurse who had brought the capsules and wished to arrange times for the physiotherapy. Bertram was now free to leave the hospital.

'Chief Inspector,' he said irritably – the pain was disturbing him – 'Your questions will have to wait. I'm going home.'

'How are you off for transport?' Tansey looked at Daphne. 'Perhaps I could drive you.'

'That would be wonderful.' She smiled her gratitude. 'The van was out delivering when the police phoned to tell me about Bertram, and I got the chap who runs the garage at Little Chipping to bring me in. It was the quickest way.'

Tansey accepted the explanation. He didn't ask why she hadn't appealed to Charlbury Hall; he was well aware that Bertram didn't like receiving favours, especially from Christopher Portman.

'Fine,' Tansey said. 'Shall we go, then.'

During the drive, he told them what Bernard Osterly had said, some of which was new to Bertram, who denied having heard a motorbike. Daphne was not surprised.

'I guessed it would be something like that,' she said. 'This character's never going to let up. He watches us like a hawk. He doesn't seem to care how much time or energy he wastes spying on us, waiting for us to be vulnerable. He'll go on till you put him behind bars, Chief Inspector.'

'And there doesn't seem much prospect of that.' Bertram was bitter.

'Bertram!' Daphne protested. 'The chief inspector can't work miracles.'

'I only wish I could,' Tansey said.

When he got back to Kidlington, Tansey, slightly piqued by Bertram's comment, decided to waste no more time.

After a late lunch he returned to his office and put through a call to the Peebles police. Having identified himself, he explained that he wanted to get in touch with Edmund Carton, believed to be living with his sister, Mrs Elizabeth Randelson. He gave the address and telephone number and asked if the local police could help, as he had been unable to contact Mr Carton, and the matter was urgent.

There was silence at the other end of the line, and at the moment when he was about to ask if the officer was still there, a different voice with a broad Scottish accent said, 'I'm afraid you're too late, sir. Obviously you don't know.'

'Know what?' Tansey demanded.

'Mr Edmund Carton killed himself, sir. Must have been shortly after Easter. His poor sister found him hanging from the stair rail when she returned from shopping one Saturday morning. It was a dreadful blow for the poor lady. She thought the world of her brother. Devoted to him, she was. She gave up her job at the library when he came to live with her and . . .'

Tansey was no longer listening. It was the timing that had struck him. Approximately three months ago Edmund Carton had committed suicide, time for Jocelyn Hauler to absorb the fact of his friend's death, which without doubt was the direct result of the loss of Frankie whom they had both loved; time to decide on revenge. But had Jocelyn Hauler known that Carton had killed himself? It was not unreasonable that Beth Randelson should have written to tell him but, if so, he had hidden his feelings extremely well when he was being questioned.

'. . . poor woman,' the Peebles officer was continuing. 'She's away at present. I know, because she asked us to keep an eye on her house. She's gone down to somewhere near you – Colombury in Oxfordshire. It must be part of your patch. Her brother used to live there. She's his executor and she has to arrange for his house and its contents to be sold. I gather it has been let furnished, but the tenants have left. So if you'd like to talk to her – '

'Yes. You're quite right. If she's in Colombury I can easily go and call on her. Far more satisfactory than telephoning. Very many thanks.'

'A pleasure, sir. We're always ready to help people in the south.'

But what you've actually done, Tansey said to himself, is to annihilate my chief suspect, indeed my only suspect apart from Jocelyn Hauler, unless –

It was a very thoughtful chief inspector who spent the afternoon going through the files and his notes on the interviews with all the individuals concerned in the case. And by the time he had locked up his papers and decided to go home, his suspicion that Frankie Carton's death had not directly triggered the attacks on the inhabitants of Wychwood Manor had given way to a near certainty, though he was convinced that more of the story remained to be unravelled.

18

Why? Why? Tansey asked himself as he drove to Headquarters the following morning. He was depressed about his
lack of progress in the case, and it was a dank day that
promised rain – the kind of day that encouraged gloomy
thoughts. Why? he asked himself again. What was the
motive? It had to be revenge. It had all the hallmarks of
revenge, the seeming need to frighten, to increase the pressure of fear, to toy with the victims' feelings, like a cat playing
with a mouse before the final pounce. The final pounce?
When was that to come? What form might it take? And
could it be avoided?

On an impulse, instead of going to his office, Tansey
decided to go to Abingdon and pay another visit to Jocelyn
Hauler, for if the desire for revenge was not in some way
connected with Frankie Carton's death, he had no idea of its
cause.

Again, the shop was empty of visitors, but this time the
owner was present in addition to Hauler. Ezekiel Dale was
as glossy, as cared for and as tenderly preserved as any of
his books, and he looked as old. In a grey alpaca jacket and
black trousers, he was the perfect picture of an antiquarian
bookseller.

But if his appearance suggested that he was past his sell-by
date, his mind certainly was not. He quickly grasped that
Tansey was seeking an alibi for Hauler, who had irritably
denied being a witness to the fictitious accident that Tansey
had invented.

'Let me see,' said the old man. 'Let me see. The office diary
might be able to help us. I think we were both here all day.

I'm sure the books I'd bought from that sale at Banbury had just arrived and – '

He excused himself and pottered into a back room. Hauler said quickly, 'What's this all about, Chief Inspector? I don't understand. You can't possibly believe – '

'Please.' Tansey held up a warning hand as Mr Dale returned to the shop.

Dale peered at the open diary he was carrying. 'Yes. I was right. Here we are.' He passed the book to Tansey. 'Look for yourself, Chief Inspector.'

Tansey didn't know whether to be pleased or sorry. On the day Daphne Mariner had been thrust into shelves of soup cans by a shopping trolley – the day Tansey had given on this occasion for his fictitious accident – Jocelyn Hauler had not been in Colombury. And this attack had to have been spontaneous. The situation didn't clear Hauler completely; he could, as had occurred to Tansey earlier, have been paying someone to persecute the Rocques, and the man might – just might – have acted on his own initiative. But this seemed most unlikely.

'. . . beautiful books,' Mr Dale was saying. 'A tragedy such a library had to be broken up. We had a wonderful time unpacking them, so wonderful we forgot all about lunch, and it wasn't till after two that Jocelyn popped out to get some sandwiches for us.'

Ezekiel Dale smiled apologetically at Tansey, and Tansey smiled in return. He knew little about books, valuable or otherwise, but he could appreciate enthusiastic expertise when he saw it. He said how sorry he was to have wasted Mr Dale's – and Mr Hauler's – time.

'Time!' Dale said unexpectedly, looking at his watch. 'I promised to make a phone call. If you'll excuse me, Chief Inspector, Jocelyn will see you out.'

And most opportunely he disappeared into the back room, leaving Tansey alone with Hauler. Tansey, who had been wondering how he could get Hauler to himself for a few minutes, was relieved.

He said, 'Mr Hauler, I have some bad news for you.'

'Bad news?'

'Yes. Your friend, Edmund Carton – you said you hadn't heard from him since Easter. I'm afraid he's dead.'

'Dead! How did he die? He was a young man – comparatively. Was it his heart? Or an accident?' Hauler collapsed on to a chair. There was no questioning the genuineness of his surprise.

'You didn't know?'

'No, how should I have known?'

'His sister didn't write to you?'

'No!' Hauler snapped. 'What happened?' he demanded, surprise giving way to anger. 'Tell me, damn it! How did Edmund die?'

'He took his own life, Mr Hauler, not long after Easter. He hanged himself.'

'Oh no! Poor Edmund! He ought never to have gone to live with that bitch of a sister of his. She wouldn't have known how to sympathize with him. She never understood what Frankie's death meant to him.' Once Hauler had started to speak it seemed as if he couldn't stop.

He went on, 'I don't believe she cared a damn about Frankie. Her own marriage hadn't lasted long – Edmund told me her husband walked out on her – and they didn't have any children. He said she didn't really like children, or know how to deal with them, which is why when Edmund's wife, Margaret, died, he refused to take Frankie to live with her. He was sure the boy wouldn't be happy there. Personally, I think she was jealous of Frankie. She resented anyone, me included, who was at all close to Edmund.'

The stream of words stopped as abruptly as it had begun, and Hauler made a gesture of helpless resignation. Tansey was staring at him, his thoughts elsewhere. He was remembering that the police officer at Peebles had said that Mrs Randelson had been devoted to her brother, and now Hauler had confirmed it beyond doubt.

Then the old man returned. 'Still with us, Chief Inspector?'

'Just going,' Tansey said. He looked directly at Hauler. 'Many thanks for your help. Goodbye.'

*　　*　　*

Tansey drove on from Abingdon to Colombury but, nearing the outskirts, instead of going into the town, turned up the lane to the small house where Frankie Carton had lived. It looked exactly as it had done on his previous visit, except that what appeared to be a brand new car was parked in front. Indeed, when he got out of his own car he saw it was a this year's model, and that the sticker on its back window read 'Windrush Garage'.

'Good morning,' a voice said. 'Can I help you?'

A woman had come out of the house. She was about fifty and grey-haired, but with a neat figure and, as she bent down to pull out an offending weed and then advanced towards him, Tansey registered that she had a supple athletic body that belied her apparent age. He introduced himself.

'Oh dear!' she said. 'I was hoping you might be someone interested in buying the house.'

'No, this is a police inquiry, Mrs Randelson. I'm right? You are Mrs Elizabeth Randelson?' He produced his warrant card, which she inspected carefully.

'Yes, I'm Elizabeth Randelson, but – What's this about, Chief Inspector? I'm sure I haven't been speeding and, even if I had, it wouldn't warrant a visit from an officer of your rank.'

'This is a more serious matter than speeding, Mrs Randelson. I had hoped to speak to Mr Edmund Carton, but –'

'My brother is dead!'

It was as if a shutter had come down over a pleasant, open face. Tansey felt repulsed. He remembered how Jocelyn Hauler had stressed Beth Randelson's devotion to her brother – obsessive, in his view – and how this had been to some extent corroborated by the police officer in Peebles. And he also remembered once again the thought that had occurred to him when he parted from Hauler.

But Mrs Randelson had recovered quickly. 'You'd better come in, Chief Inspector. Perhaps I can help you after all.'

In the sitting-room, she waved him to a chair and sat opposite him, her back to the light. She picked up some knitting from a nearby table, and started to knit, giving him a smile over the clicking needles.

'Now, Chief Inspector,' she said encouragingly.

'There is renewed interest in the death last autumn of your nephew, Mrs Randelson,' Tansey began.

'Really? Poor little Frankie's death?' she replied, without any apparent emotion. She waited, making no further comment.

'If you'd be prepared to cast your mind back to last January,' said Tansey.

'January?' She was surprised.

'I believe you were staying here then, helping your brother to prepare the house for tenants, before he went back to Scotland with you.'

'That's right, Chief Inspector. You're well informed.' Beth Randelson sounded amused. 'I must say I can't imagine how that might interest the police.'

'Your brother received an anonymous letter at that time, claiming to describe the car that had knocked down and killed his son, and naming its owner. Did he show you this letter, Mrs Randelson?'

Beth Randelson stopped knitting. 'Indeed he didn't, Chief Inspector. My brother's opinion of anonymous letters was the same as mine. They are not to be trusted. The best thing to do with them is to tear them up and throw them away.'

'Or throw them into the fire and let them burn,' Tansey suggested and, when this remark brought no response, added, 'But your brother told you about this particular letter, didn't he, Mrs Randelson? After all, the subject was terribly important to him.'

'No, I'm afraid he didn't – tell me about it, I mean. So I can't help you, Chief Inspector.' Beth Randelson took up her knitting again; she seemed quite composed. 'I admit it does surprise me that Edmund never mentioned the contents of such a letter. Perhaps he didn't receive it. May I ask who your authority is? I suppose it wasn't that young man, one of Frankie's teachers at Coriston, Jocelyn Hauler?'

'Yes. Actually, it was.'

'Oh well! I don't think he's a very reliable character, Chief Inspector. He was not a good influence on Frankie, or probably on any impressionable boy, if you follow what I would prefer not to state explicitly.'

'You didn't like him?'

'I scarcely knew him, but after Frankie was killed he was always coming around here, supposedly to give Edmund support — support he didn't need while I was in the house.'

'Then you never let him know that your brother had been so unhappy that he had taken his own life — in fact, that he had hanged himself?'

There was a sharp click, like the breaking of a bone. Beth Randelson, her face set, was looking down at the knitting in her lap. One of her needles had snapped. She bundled her work together and put it on the table beside her.

'No, Chief Inspector! I did not let him know of my brother's death. It was none of his business.'

Tansey nodded; there was nothing more he could say. Deliberately he looked at his watch and then stood up. 'I won't keep you any longer, Mrs Randelson. If I hear of anyone interested in buying the house, I'll let you know.'

The awkward moment had passed. Beth Randelson saw Tansey to the door. It had eventually become a fairly clear day, but now the weather had changed again. The sky had clouded over and rain was beginning to fall.

'Oh, I must put the car away,' she said. 'It's not mine. I hired it from the local garage. I came down to Colombury by train. It's too far for an old woman like me to drive, but one needs transport of some kind here. This house is a couple of miles from the little town, as you must know.'

'It's certainly easier to make the journey from Scotland by train, rather than by car,' Tansey agreed, discounting the suggestion that Beth Randelson was 'an old woman'. 'Let me open your garage door for you,' he volunteered.

'Thank you. It *is* a heavy door.'

Tansey swung the door up and over, and stood back to let Mrs Randelson drive into the garage, which she did neatly and efficiently. He waited until she had got out of the car, and then swung the door down for her.

'I see you have a motorbike,' he said conversationally. 'Do you ride it?'

'Heavens, no! That old thing belonged to my brother. He didn't own a car. He wasn't a rich man, Chief Inspector, and what extra money he had he spent on the boy.'

Tansey made no comment. He thanked her once more, said goodbye and drove down the lane, conscious that Beth Randelson was watching him.

'Chief Inspector, your evidence is totally circumstantial,' said Philip Midvale.

'I know that, sir,' Tansey agreed.

They were in the chief constable's office and Tansey was explaining how, he believed, the reckless killing of Frankie Carton had led to Edmund Carton's suicide from grief at the loss of his son, and subsequently to the frightening and increasingly serious persecution of Wychwood Manor and its inhabitants.

'Nevertheless,' he persisted, 'it's the only explanation that fits, sir.'

'Are you sure you haven't adjusted the pieces to suit your theory, Chief Inspector?'

'I don't believe so, sir.'

'Supposing you're right, Chief Inspector, what hope have you of getting any proof? Take Frankie's death first. Even if this man Brail were a respectable character, his evidence is worthless. He can't swear that the Toyota he saw at the scene of the hit-and-run was the same one he saw Portman driving later; he didn't take the licence number and by now the Rocques' Toyota has been resprayed so often that the paint left on Frankie's bike couldn't possibly be identified with it. So, where's your proof? Don't expect Portman to admit Andrea Rocque was driving and killed the boy, because I'm prepared to bet he won't. Anyway, why are you so sure Portman wasn't driving himself?'

'Because it would have been out of character for him not to have stopped, but Lady Rocque has a reputation for driving too fast, and she gets tipsy on occasion. However, it's all academic now, sir. I'm not interested in prosecuting Lady Rocque for manslaughter. Frankie's dead, and so is his father.

That can't be undone. I merely want to prevent a third tragedy.'

'All right, Chief Inspector. Let's assume Lady Rocque killed Frankie, and turn to the persecution of the Rocques.' Midvale was curter than usual, but he had a lot on his mind; there had been several horrific crimes involving murder, rape and arson on his patch recently, most still unsolved. 'Do you really believe a fifty-year-old woman could conceivably be responsible?'

'Yes, sir. You've not met Mrs Elizabeth Randelson. She's an active woman, and a determined character. She's had the time; the attacks started after she left Peebles. She's not unfamiliar with the district; she's stayed at Carton's house a number of times. She's had opportunity; she's been living alone, and answerable to nobody. She has the means, the suspected transport – the motorbike I saw in her garage. It probably is Carton's, but it's no dusty, neglected object: it's clean, and with a clean black full crash helmet hanging on the handlebars. Above all, sir, she has a motive: revenge – not for the death of Frankie, but for the death of her brother, to whom she was obsessively attached, and which resulted indirectly from the killing of Frankie.'

'Anything else?'

'She lied about the anonymous letter, even suggesting that Jocelyn Hauler invented it, which we know he didn't. I believe her brother did tell her about it. Possibly because he resented her curiosity he mentioned only Sir Bertram Rocque's name, which is why there have been no attacks on Mr Portman, or just possibly she found some bits of the letter unburnt in the grate.'

Midvale shifted uncomfortably in his chair and shook his head. 'Well, you've certainly made out a case, Chief Inspector, but it's either circumstantial or supposition. You haven't a scrap of concrete proof of Mrs Randelson's responsibility. If you pulled her in, she'd laugh in your face and probably accuse you of false arrest.'

'Then what do you suggest I do, sir?' Tansey did his best to hide his annoyance, and his disappointment.

'I don't think there's anything you can do, except hope

that if you're right and she is the guilty party, your questions today may have deterred her from further action.'

'Yes, sir,' Tansey said. What else could he say? You don't argue with your chief constable. But he was not optimistic, and he wished he could hazard a guess as to what Beth Randelson might be planning next.

19

The rest of the week passed quietly. Bertram Rocque went into Colombury daily by bus, or van if it was available, for physiotherapy on his shoulder. He refused to go in the Ford which Christopher Portman had insisted on lending Daphne. On Thursday, Simon Wayne collected the Toyota, more dilapidated than ever, from Field's garage, and swapped it for the Ford. At Christopher's instigation he had taken to dropping in at the Manor in Bertram's absence, but there was really little he could do to help Daphne. They were all on edge, waiting, but there were no more 'incidents'.

On Sunday, Andrea Rocque put through a telephone call from Spain to Charlbury Hall and asked to speak to Mr Portman. Simon answered the phone and said that Christopher was not available. Andrea didn't believe him. 'Simon, don't be obstructive! I asked to speak to Chris, and it's Chris I want to speak to, not you.'

'I'm sorry, Andrea, but, as I said, Chris is *not* available at present.'

'On a Sunday morning? Don't tell me he's gone to church.'

'Surprisingly, yes. He has two business colleagues and their wives staying for the weekend. They are Swiss, from Geneva, Protestants, and as they expressed a wish to attend church, he has taken them to St Matthew's at Little Chipping.'

'Very well. Tell him I'll phone again around lunch time.'

Andrea Rocque cut the connection between her and Simon Wayne before he could respond, and he swore softly. He hoped this call wasn't to announce her return from Spain; he had enjoyed her absence, the more so as Christopher had shown no sign of missing her. And later, when he duly delivered her message, he was pleased that Christopher didn't attempt to phone back immediately, but waited for her call.

'Andrea's returning on Tuesday,' Christopher murmured to Simon as he escorted his guests in to lunch. 'She wanted me to meet her at Heathrow.'

'That wouldn't be inconvenient. You'll be in London,' Simon said, hiding his disappointment at the news. 'If you don't want to go out to the airport yourself you can always send Sutton with the car.'

'No, we might need it ourselves. I told Andrea that unfortunately it was impossible.' Christopher turned to the wife of his more important guest. 'My apologies. We were talking about a neighbour,' he said, as if Andrea Rocque had never meant anything to him.

Andrea would not have been pleased to hear this casual dismissal of her as a mere 'neighbour', and anyway she was not in the best of tempers. She considered that Christopher had been too offhand about his refusal to meet her at the airport. She phoned Wychwood Manor next, and was glad that it was her husband who answered.

'Tuesday, darling? That's great,' Bertram said. 'We weren't expecting you so soon. There's nothing wrong, is there?'

'No. I've just got bored here,' Andrea lied.

In fact, Marlene Sinclair, stating as an excuse that they had relatives coming to stay unexpectedly, had asked her to cut short her visit. The real reason, Andrea knew, was that one evening she had drunk a little too much, and had unwisely flirted with Marlene's step-son, whose wife had objected.

'That's a pity, but it'll be good to have you home again, darling.'

'It's *getting* home that's the problem, Bertram. Unless you can meet me at Heathrow I don't know how I'll manage. I've so much luggage.'

'Andrea, there's nothing I'd like more than to meet you at Heathrow, but I'm not able to drive at present. I've hurt my shoulder and a trip to London would be impossible.'

'What about Daphne?'

'Daphne?' Bertram glanced across the room at his sister, who shook her head violently. 'No, Andrea. I'm sorry, darling. Daphne's busy on Tuesday.'

'You could send Jimmy with our van,' Daphne said, suppressing a smile. 'It would cope with the luggage.'

'I heard that,' Andrea said sharply, not sure if Daphne had been serious. Anyhow, she was not going to be fobbed off with a rather derelict van and a delivery man for a driver. 'Obviously I'm a nuisance, so don't bother! I'll make my own way.' And you can pay for the taxis and the first class train fare from Paddington, she added under her breath. 'Goodbye till Tuesday, Bertram.'

The week had not been a good one for Chief Inspector Tansey either. The more he thought about Beth Randelson the more certain he was that she had been responsible for the attacks on the Rocques' property and persons, and the more certain he became that she was not yet satisfied that her brother's death had been avenged. He believed that she looked upon Edmund Carton's death almost as a personal affront. By depriving Edmund of his son and thus causing him to take his life, the guilty party had deprived her of the one person she loved – and therefore must pay for it. Beth Randelson, Tansey was sure, was a determined and dangerous woman.

If the week was trying, the weekend without the distraction of office work was worse. He mowed the lawn. He watched Hilary bath the baby. He read his small son to sleep. He helped wash up the supper dishes. But all the time he was wondering about the Randelson woman, and who was most in danger from her. Daphne Mariner was the obvious choice, but in the circumstances he could think of no way of giving her more protection – and then, of course, there were Portman and Wayne.

At ten, Hilary decided to go to bed, but Tansey said he wasn't feeling sleepy. She looked at him in exasperation.

'Dick, what's the matter? You've been like a cat on hot bricks all the weekend, when you should be relaxing, resting, storing up energy for the week ahead.'

'Yes. I'll need a lot of energy sitting at my desk and pushing papers around.'

'Is that the trouble? Midvale's taken you off the case?'

'It would be easier if he had. No, he just wants me to wait and see, basically because he doesn't trust my findings. But it's just not logical. If I'm in the wrong, nothing will be achieved by inaction, and if I'm in the right, someone's probably going to get killed.' Tansey sighed. 'I can't make up my mind what to do,' he admitted.

Hilary bent over and kissed him. 'Back your own judgement, Dick,' she said.

And when she had gone to bed Tansey no longer hesitated. He went to the telephone, tapped out the number of Charlbury Hall and arranged to call on Christopher Portman the next morning.

'Mr Portman, Mr Wayne,' Tansey said. 'I'm going to tell you "off the record" who I believe is responsible for these attacks on the Rocques, and why they've been taking place. The chief constable doesn't accept my analysis and won't act on it, so by coming to you I'm risking my job. However, I hope you will take what I say as confidential.'

And he proceeded to tell them what he knew and believed about Elizabeth Randelson, in the same terms as those he had used to Midvale. 'I think she's obsessed with the idea of revenge,' he concluded, 'which is why I'm giving you a serious warning to be on your guard, and not invite an attack. It's possible she doesn't know of your connection, Mr Portman. Her brother may not have mentioned your name, or that part of Brail's letter to him could have been burnt. It's also possible either of you could be next on her list.'

'So no more solitary walks for the present, Simon,' Portman said, only half joking. Both he and Wayne had listened to Tansey in silence and this was the first comment either of them had made.

'But what about the people at the Manor, Chief Inspector? They're far more vulnerable than we are. Incidentally,' he added, 'Andrea Rocque's coming back from Spain tomorrow.'

175

'That's bad news in the circumstances, sir,' Tansey said. 'Of course, I intend to stress to them that the incidents are probably not over yet and they must take precautions. But it would be impossible to explain to either Sir Bertram or Lady Rocque about Mrs Randelson without mentioning Frankie, and I'm sure you'll appreciate that's not feasible. However, I believed it important to tell you, because I've always believed that knowing the identity of the enemy gives one an advantage. I hoped you would understand.'

'Of course, Chief Inspector – we're grateful – and those aren't just conventional words,' Portman said. 'The whole thing's a mess, and I'm certainly partially responsible.' He paused; it was the nearest he got to admitting to Tansey that the chief inspector's version of Frankie Carton's death was correct. 'But I would ask you a favour.'

'What, sir?'

'I would like to tell Daphne – Mrs Mariner – what you've just told us. Someone at the Manor should know the form if this crazy character is likely to launch another attack, and Mrs Mariner's a level-headed woman who can be trusted. Moreover, I'm afraid she's in the greatest danger.'

Tansey thought for a moment. Then, 'Certainly, sir. But please stress to her the necessity of keeping the full story to herself. As I said, I'll give Sir Bertram a general warning that his troubles are probably not at an end, and ask him to impress on his wife the need for great care. I regret there's nothing else to be done at the moment.'

'Except hope and pray,' said Portman.

Later in the morning Christopher Portman drove over to Wychwood Manor. He had an excuse ready – an invitation to Sunday lunch to celebrate Andrea's return – but he was in luck: Daphne was alone; Bertram had gone into Colombury for a physiotherapy session.

Having delivered the invitation, Portman said, 'Daphne, I had a more important reason for this visit than asking you all to lunch. I wanted to make a clandestine date with you so that we could have a long, serious talk. However, now's an excellent time for it, if you'll abandon that damned hoeing.'

'Does it concern those attacks on us? Chief Inspector Tansey looked in to warn us that they may not be over yet and we should be on our guard. I promised to pass his message on to Bertram and Andrea, not that there's much we can do about it, really.'

'Yes, it does concern these attacks, Daphne,' Portman said. 'I'm afraid there's a lot you don't know yet. I asked Tansey if I might tell you his – his theory, and he agreed. It all started with Andrea, the day of the Sinclair–Jowett wedding in Chipping Norton.'

Christopher Portman didn't spare himself or try to make excuses. He impressed on Daphne the need for complete confidentiality, and then told her the whole story, the hit-and-run accident that had caused Frankie Carton's death, Brail's attempt at blackmail and how that had been frustrated, Brail's anonymous letter to Edmund Carton, Elizabeth Randelson's jealous love of her brother, his suicide and her apparent determination that his death should be avenged.

'And you believe this theory of the chief inspector's, Chris?'

'Yes. I'd be prepared to trust Tansey. He's intelligent and perceptive. If he'd like to leave the police I wouldn't mind giving him a job.'

'High praise coming from you.' Daphne was amused. 'But seriously, Chris, it's not a pleasant situation we're in, is it? Can't anything be done? I feel sorry for this woman; she must be mentally disturbed. I wish to God the little boy hadn't been killed and her brother hadn't committed suicide, but destroying us won't bring them back. If only she'd go away and leave us alone. We've enough problems without her adding to them.'

'I know. It's a pity I can't deal with her as I dealt with Brail but it simply isn't practical, and anyway Tansey wouldn't stand for it.'

They went on to discuss Andrea's return the next day, and the invitation to Sunday lunch at the Hall. Christopher drove off home, and Daphne went back to her hoeing, wondering when the next disaster would strike and how much longer they could go on in this state of fearful anticipation, pretending that life was normal.

Andrea Rocque returned the following day. She arrived at Wychwood Manor by taxi, which she left Bertram to pay while with Daphne's help she carried her bags, including a new holdall, into the hall. She looked brown and healthy and rested, fully recovered from her accident with the bolting mare. Daphne, who was feeling tired and out of sorts, envied her.

'Dear old England,' Andrea said, throwing her light raincoat over a chair. 'Grey skies and showers, umbrella weather.'

'Actually, darling, it's been quite good while you've been away,' Bertram protested, 'though not compared with Spain, I suppose. Leave your bags for the moment, and come and have a drink and tell us about it. Did you enjoy yourself?'

'Moderately.'

'Only moderately?'

'Well, it's no fun being the poor relation. The Sinclairs are terribly kind and so are their friends, but it's embarrassing not to be able to offer to pay for a round of drinks or go shares in a meal occasionally. Even the maids looked askance at the small tips I left them, but I couldn't afford any more.'

'Darling, I'm sorry, but –'

'You managed to buy yourself a few things, I see,' Daphne interrupted; she wasn't sure which she hated more – Andrea's blatant selfishness or Bertram's subservient acceptance of it.

'One or two. Trifles.' Andrea smothered a yawn. 'Lord, I'm exhausted. I had a dreadful journey. I think I'll postpone the drink. I'll go to my room, unpack, have a shower and a rest before dinner.'

'That's a good idea,' Bertram said. 'Daphne, you'll help with the bags, won't you? My shoulder –'

'Yes, how is your poor shoulder, Bertram? I meant to ask. And have there been any more of those unpleasant incidents?'

178

'No, darling, but that doesn't mean we shouldn't be vigilant.'

'In fact, Chief Inspector Tansey believes we should be extra careful after this quiet period,' Daphne said. She picked up a couple of bags. 'Come on, Andrea. Let's get you sorted out.'

'You're always so efficient,' Andrea said rather plaintively as they went upstairs.

She meant the comment to be a compliment, and Daphne swallowed the remark that one of them had to be efficient. The phone started to ring as they reached the bedroom, and Andrea ran to answer it.

'It could be Chris,' she said over her shoulder. 'Hello! Andrea Rocque here.' The next moment she flung the receiver on to the bed. 'It's him again, with his threats.'

'What?'

Daphne seized the receiver, and heard a voice say, '. . . pay for your sins.' She was in no doubt who was on the line and, angry, almost without thinking, she snapped, 'You wretched woman, if you don't stop persecuting us you'll go to prison for a long time. The police know who you are, Randelson, and one more –' She stopped. The line had gone dead.

Andrea had collapsed into a chair and was hiding her face in her hands. She appeared not to have heard or, at any rate, not to have understood what Daphne had been saying.

'Oh God!' she said. 'It's started again. What are we going to do? I wish I'd never come back to this place.'

'It's your home and your husband's home.' Daphne was not in a conciliatory mood. 'Try thinking about Bertram a bit more, Andrea, rather than yourself,' she said, and marched out of the room leaving Andrea to her thoughts.

In the small house outside Colombury where Edmund Carton had once lived with his son Frankie, Beth Randelson sat and stared at the telephone. She was shaking and there was a thin veil of sweat on her face. She didn't know who had seized the phone and threatened her by name, but she guessed it was Bertram Rocque's sister.

Anyway, it didn't matter. They knew who she was, thanks to that damned policeman; that was the important point.

179

She had been distraught ever since the day he had come to see her, to ask questions about that piece of unburnt letter naming Rocque that she had rescued from the fire. She had denied all knowledge of it, but clearly he hadn't believed her, not after she had been fool enough to let him see the motorbike in the garage. She wiped her face with the back of her hand. She didn't care what happened to her personally. They could send her to prison if they liked. But she hadn't finished with the task she had undertaken – to avenge dear Edmund's death – and now it seemed there might not be much time left in which to achieve it.

20

Sunday, and at Charlbury Hall Christopher Portman was awaiting his luncheon guests. It was to be a small party, Andrea and Bertram, Daphne, Simon and himself, with the main intention of cheering everyone up a little. He had thought of inviting two or three other people, but had decided against it. When he was not entertaining for business reasons or particular celebrations, he preferred to have informal, relaxed meals with friends.

The invitation had been for twelve-thirty, but it was not until ten to one that Simon, looking up from the newspaper he was reading, commented on the tardiness of the expected guests. 'Are you sure you didn't say one o'clock, Chris?'

'I'm pretty sure, though I must admit my mind was on other things.'

'So was Daphne's, probably, and afterwards she may have thought you'd said one.'

Simon returned to his newspaper and Christopher to his book. The clock on the mantel struck the hour and they exchanged glances. But it was fifteen minutes later before either of them expressed any anxiety.

Then Christopher said, 'Where the hell are they? Even if they thought it was one o'clock they're still late.'

'Something must have held them up.'

'They could have phoned.'

'Would you like me to phone the Manor and see if they've left yet?'

'No. Let's wait till half past. I suppose they might have had a flat. If we phone and they have already left, it'll only worry old Alice.'

Christopher got to his feet and started to walk up and down the room. The minutes ticked by, the tick of the clock sounding depressingly loud. Simon folded his newspaper and laid it on the table beside him.

'For heaven's sake, Chris, do stop your pacing. It's making me nervous.'

'I'm already nervous.' Christopher flung himself into a chair. 'If anything's happened – Simon, there's something I have to tell you and I might as well do it now. It's relevant because of who might be involved if there has been another incident or accident. I – I'm planning to get married.'

'What?' Simon was unbelieving.

'You heard. I'm planning to get married – as soon as possible, I hope. I should have got round to it a long time ago. I don't know why I didn't. Anyhow, it's not too late. If we can't have children of our own, maybe we can adopt a couple.'

'Chris!' Simon protested. 'How much thought have you given this? Have you considered how different your life will be? And what about Bertram? You know how dependent he is on her.'

'He'll have to get used to it, Simon. Of course, it will mean changes for him – and for me, but –'

'For me, too, Chris.' Simon was suddenly crisp. 'If you've really made up your mind then I'm afraid I shall be leaving you. I'll give you time to find a replacement, of course, and do my best to break him in for you, but after that I'll go.'

'Simon, you can't!' Christopher was aghast. 'It never occurred to me – I never thought you'd take it like this. I thought you'd congratulate me, be happy for me.'

'I'm sorry. I can't. I wish I could, but I think you're making a bad mistake.'

'I know that your own marriage was a disaster, but that doesn't mean –'

There was a tap at the door, and the houseman came in carrying a telephone. 'A call for you, sir. From Wychwood Manor. It's Alice, the housekeeper. She sounds very upset.'

'All right. Thanks.' Christopher grabbed the phone. 'Hello,

Alice. Christopher Portman speaking. Is there some trouble, my dear?' He listened intently.

To Simon, who heard only brief interjections from Christopher, such as 'Are the police still there?' and 'How badly?', the one-sided conversation seemed interminable. Moreover, he couldn't remember seeing Christopher look so grim, and when he put the phone down he didn't speak at once, but stared unseeingly into the distance. Simon, yearning to know what had happened, had the greatest difficulty in remaining silent.

Then, after a long minute, Christopher said, 'They were on their way here. It was a head-on collision. Sergeant Donaldson recognized Bertram and sent WPC Digby to warn Alice there had been a serious accident, and get her to inform anyone else who — who should be informed.'

'Which means it really is extremely serious.'

'Yes. How serious I don't know, but they're all badly hurt. They've been taken to the hospital in Colombury, the three of them, and the woman driving the other car.'

'At least they're alive, so there's hope. Chris, I'll get the car.'

It was not until they were in the car that Christopher spoke again. He picked up the carphone and got through to the headquarters of the Thames Valley Police Force at Kidlington.

'I want Chief Inspector Tansey . . . Oh. Well, this is Christopher Portman. Tell the chief inspector to get details of an accident involving Sir Bertram Rocque from Sergeant Donaldson at Colombury, and then phone me. I'll be at Colombury hospital . . . Many thanks . . . Tell him it's urgent.'

Simon had listened in some surprise. 'Tansey! Why?'

'This was no accident, Simon. The police told Alice the name of the woman driving the other car. Evidently they got it from her driving licence.' Christopher's voice was taut. 'It's Elizabeth Randelson.'

On a Sunday afternoon, the hospital was buzzing with visitors bringing flowers and fruit, and children come to see grandma or auntie. The place was short staffed. The last thing anyone had wanted was an accident in the neighbourhood involving four serious casualties. Emergency was stretched. Already they had a man who had fallen off a ladder and a boy who had swallowed some cleaning fluid. There seemed to be no one prepared to answer questions.

But Christopher Portman was not to be denied, certainly not when he was as determined as he now was. In exasperation, he told the receptionist that he was expecting a phone call from Chief Inspector Tansey of the Thames Valley Police about certain patients and she had better see he had some answers ready. After which it was not long before he and Simon were being shown by a porter into the office of the senior matron, a small beak-nosed woman who radiated quiet efficiency.

'Mr Portman, Mr Wayne,' she greeted them. 'Perhaps you would explain your relationship to the accident victims, and why you're threatening us with the police.'

'We're close friends and neighbours of the Rocques and Mrs Mariner, Matron, and extremely concerned about them. Mrs Randelson we've never met. And I'm certainly not "threatening" you with the police. It's a long and complex story, and the police are already very much involved. All I've done is cut through red tape, and attempt to contact the officer who has been investigating various related incidents. Now perhaps you'll tell me how the patients are, and then I'll explain further if necessary.'

'Very well. I regret to say that Sir Bertram is dead. He was dead on arrival here. Lady Rocque is suffering from shock, bruising, cuts – that applies to all the survivors – but she has no obvious broken bones and I think it's safe to assume she's in no danger. She's under sedation and hasn't yet been told of her husband's death.'

'And Mrs Mariner?'

'More serious. She was driving. She's still unconscious. She has a crushed ribcage and probably internal injuries. That's all I can tell you at the moment. We'll know more when the X-rays are completed. Then we'll have to decide whether to transfer her to Oxford.'

'It's as bad as that?'

184

'Maybe. Now, as for Mrs Randelson – but you're not interested in her –'

'Oh, yes we are!' Christopher Portman said hoarsely. 'We couldn't be more interested.'

Matron looked at him curiously. 'I don't understand. You said you'd never met her.' She shrugged. 'In any case, Mrs Randelson is a very sick woman. She has dreadful injuries. We must always hope, of course, but the prognosis is not good. She's not expected to survive.'

The telephone on the desk burred. Matron answered it and at once passed the instrument to Christopher Portman. There was no need for her to say who was on the line, and Portman gave Tansey a brief account of events as he believed them to be before returning the phone to Matron. She listened intently to Tansey's instructions that a constant watch was to be kept on Mrs Randelson until a police guard could be provided.

The precaution was unnecessary. At two o'clock in the morning PC Wright, who was half asleep on the hard wooden chair beside Beth Randelson's bed, was startled by a sudden cry from her.

'Edmund!' she cried. 'Edmund!'

Wright rang for the nurse, but Beth Randelson never regained consciousness and, soon after calling her brother's name, she died without the consolation of knowing that she had exacted vengeance, though from a man who was completely innocent.

Beth Randelson was not to claim any other victims. Daphne was not as seriously hurt as had at first been suspected, and was not evacuated to Oxford. By the afternoon of the following day, having been told of Bertram's death, she was transferred from the Intensive Care Unit to a two-bedded room where Andrea was already ensconced. It was not an ideal arrangement for either of them, but there was no choice, and they could scarcely suggest that sharing with a stranger, uninterested in their affairs, would have given them more privacy.

As the next several days passed, they had a steady stream

of visitors. Among the first were Chief Inspector Tansey and also the local police in the shape of Sergeant Donaldson, who was nominally investigating the 'accident'. Andrea maintained that she remembered nothing about it; her thoughts had been elsewhere, when suddenly, with a dreadful crunching sound, their car had disintegrated. Daphne, however, was convinced that the other car had driven straight at them, and the physical evidence supported her. But there was no suggestion in the media that the 'accident' had been deliberately manufactured, though the *Courier* did connect Mrs Randelson with Edmund Carton and Frankie, and the few people who knew kept it to themselves.

Mr Fenway of Fenway, Fenway & Brocklehurst, solicitors of Colombury, was among the early arrivals. Henry Fenway had dealt with Bertram Rocque's legal affairs for some years and was his executor. He proved his worth. He explained that there would be no difficulty in obtaining probate for the will; apart from a few small bequests, Andrea was the sole and residual legatee. He agreed to make all arrangements for Bertram's funeral. He went to Wychwood Manor and organized the outdoor staff. He contacted Bertram's cousin in New Zealand, though the cousin showed little interest in a title to which neither money nor property was attached. Indeed, whether it was out of a sense of duty or a feeling of friendship for Bertram, Mr Fenway did everything possible to make life easier for Bertram's widow and for Daphne.

There were other visitors, among them the vet, Peter White, and Alice, who came primarily to see Daphne, and of course Christopher Portman and Simon Wayne. Letters of sympathy at Bertram's death and get well cards arrived, and gifts of fruit and flowers. Daphne was surprised how many of them were for her.

Andrea, who before the car crash had been in excellent health after her holiday in Spain, and anyway had not been as badly hurt as Daphne, was hoping she would soon be able to leave the hospital. With the death of Mrs Randelson and the fear of any further attacks removed, she looked forward to the prospect of returning to the Manor and the pleasure of having a comfortable room to herself.

She was now allowed to be up and about, and she returned from a consultation with the doctor, to find Christopher paying a visit. 'I've just been told I can go home tomorrow,' she announced happily. 'Not that it will be home for much longer. I propose to sell the place. I don't know what your plans are, Daphne, but of course you're welcome to stay there until it's sold. Alice too. There'll be a lot of clearing up to do.'

Andrea gave Christopher a dazzling smile, which she allowed to include Daphne. She was completely unaware of the devastating effect her remarks had on them. She thought her offer generous. Mr Fenway had warned her that, although he had not had much time to look into Bertram's affairs, he didn't think she should expect too much from the estate.

'I shouldn't count on help in cleaning up from either Alice or me,' Daphne said coldly. 'Alice's friend who lives near Chipping Norton has recently been widowed and wants Alice to go and live with her. It's an excellent solution for them both. As for me, as soon as I'm able I shall be looking for a job.'

'I see. Oh well, perhaps it's for the best. I'm sure Mr Fenway will arrange some professional help for me.' Abruptly, Andrea changed the subject. 'Chris, dear, you'll come and fetch me tomorrow morning, won't you?'

'What time?'

'Ten o'clock. The hospital likes to get rid of one early.'

'All right. Ten o'clock tomorrow. I shall look forward to it. Until then, goodbye.' Christopher was already at the door and with a wave of his hand he was gone.

Andrea shook her head fondly. 'Men!' she said.

Daphne made no answer. Her eyes were tight shut and she was willing herself not to cry. She had never before felt so alone.

At five minutes to ten the next morning, Sutton, Christopher Portman's chauffeur, was escorted into the room by Matron. He bowed his head to Daphne. 'Mrs Mariner, we deeply regret poor Sir Bertram's death, but we are all so pleased you're getting better.'

'Thank you.'

He turned to Andrea. 'The car is waiting for you, my lady. Mr Portman sends his apologies, but he has an important appointment this morning and is unable to accompany you. May I take your bag?'

Andrea indicated the bag that Alice had brought for her. She was not pleased. Christopher had promised he would come. Or had he? She couldn't remember his exact words. She smiled at Daphne. 'Let me know when you've decided what you intend to do,' she said.

'Yes, of course, Andrea. Goodbye.'

'It'll be your turn to go soon, Mrs Mariner,' Matron said encouragingly.

Go where? Daphne wondered. She would have to think seriously about what she was going to do. She had a little money saved, but not much. Apart from her mother's jewellery there was nothing left of what she had inherited from her parents; it had all been swallowed up helping Bertram to support the Manor. And now there was no brother, no home.

'I must not feel sorry for myself,' she said aloud.

'Certainly not! That would be a very stupid attitude to take. And why should you?'

Daphne looked up to find Christopher laughing at her. 'Chris! Sutton said you had an appointment. Andrea's gone.'

'Good man, Sutton. He always follows my instructions to the letter.' Christopher pulled up a chair close to the bed. 'Daphne, I've been waiting to get you alone. I've come to offer you a job. You said that was what you wanted.'

'A job? At Charlbury Hall? Thank you, Chris, but no thanks! I don't want pity, and anyway it wouldn't work. I found it difficult enough living with Andrea when she was Bertram's wife, and I'm damned if –'

'Daphne! You're as bad as Simon.'

'What do you mean?'

'When I told Simon I was hoping to get married, he first tried to dissuade me, then offered me his resignation. However, when I told him it wasn't Andrea I was hoping to marry, he took it back.'

'And who are you hoping to marry?'

'Do you really need to ask, Daphne? You, of course. And not out of pity or anything. I realized some time ago how much I loved you.'

'Me! But what about Andrea?'

'Look, you know perfectly well I had an affair with Andrea. It wasn't the most sensible thing I ever did, and because she was Bertram's wife I was ashamed of it. But it's over and done with, Daphne, and it's *you* I want. I'm asking *you* to marry me. As Simon said, if I'd had any sense I'd have done it years ago. Will you marry me, darling? Please.'

'Oh, Chris! Yes.' Daphne was half laughing, half crying. 'Better late than never.'

Meanwhile, Andrea's return to Wychwood Manor was not being as pleasant as she had hoped. Alice was waiting, but not to welcome her, not to unpack her bags, not to ask if she would like coffee or what she would like for lunch. Alice was smartly dressed as if about to go out, and the hall seemed to be full of luggage.

'What's going on here?' Andrea demanded.

'I'm leaving, my lady.'

'Leaving? Right now? I thought servants usually gave notice.'

'I gave Miss Daphne notice, my lady. I believe she warned you I should be going to Chipping Norton to live with a friend of mine.'

'She did mention it, yes, but I didn't think – All right, go if you must, but don't expect me to pay you for this month.'

'Miss Daphne has already paid me. She gave me her *personal* cheque.'

'I see. And is all this your baggage?'

'No. Miss Daphne asked me to pack for her too. Mr Portman was kind enough to offer Mr Sutton's services to deliver it for us.'

'I see,' Andrea repeated.

So Daphne was going as well. She didn't ask where. She

didn't care; she didn't care. She gave a curt nod and strode off to the sitting-room. She was furiously angry. It was true that when she said she intended to sell the Manor, Daphne had told her that Alice would be leaving for Chipping Norton, and she would be leaving the Manor too, but she hadn't expected them to go so soon. And Christopher had known! That was why he had made an excuse not to fetch her from the hospital himself. She didn't understand.

Andrea poured herself a whisky. It was too early to start drinking, but she felt she needed it. She took her glass to the telephone and tapped out Henry Fenway's number, but for once Mr Fenway was not helpful. He refused her demand for a temporary cook/housekeeper on the grounds of expense. He said that he had been looking into Sir Bertram's estate, and the financial situation was even worse than he had first thought. He urged her to economize as much as possible.

Infuriated, Andrea banged down the receiver. At least once she was married to Christopher there wouldn't be any nonsense about money, but they couldn't marry at once. They would have to wait a few months for the sake of appearances. How long, she wondered. Six months? She certainly didn't intend to stay at the Manor for six months without anyone to look after her. Christopher would have to make some arrangement. Perhaps, she thought hopefully, he had already done so.

And it was with greater relief than she would have admitted that an hour later she saw Christopher Portman drive up to the house. She ran to welcome him in the hall.

'Chris! Chris, darling! I knew you'd come. It's been a bloody morning. Alice has walked out on me. Daphne's leaving the Manor too, apparently. I'd no idea this would all be happening immediately, and I don't know how I can cope by myself. You will help, won't you?'

Christopher released himself from her embrace. 'If you need help you must ask Mr Fenway, Andrea. As Bertram's executor he'll make any necessary arrangements.'

'Well — many thanks!' Andrea was angry, but also

frightened. 'Why have you come then? To tell me that now I am free you don't want to marry me?'

'Andrea, I have never suggested that I wanted to marry you. At least my conscience is clear there. We had an affair. I wish we hadn't. I'm not proud of it. However, it suited us both. It's over.'

'Over? Why? Have you found someone else?'

'I'm getting married – to Daphne.'

'Married – to Daphne?' Andrea gave a wild laugh. 'To that plain cow? You must be joking.'

'I've never been more serious.'

Andrea couldn't believe this latest blow, didn't want to believe it, but she knew it was true and temper overcame caution. 'Then – then get out of my house, you – you gardener's boy! It's what you've always wanted, isn't it? To marry a Rocque. Well, I wish you luck. You'll need it.'

Seizing a vase from the hall table Andrea flung it in Christopher's face, and as he staggered back she turned and ran upstairs. He watched her go. He felt slightly sick. Then he quickly let himself out of the house.

The following day Tansey was summoned to the chief constable's office.

'I've just had a letter from Christopher Portman, including a substantial cheque for the Police Benevolent Fund,' Midvale said. 'He expresses his thanks for my intervention in the Rocque affair, and says that you, Chief Inspector Tansey, should be complimented on the extraordinarily tactful and efficient manner in which you coped with the situation.'

'That's very kind of him, sir, but regrettably undeserved. I didn't prevent Sir Bertram's death.'

'True, but that was more my fault than yours. I should have agreed to pull Mrs Randelson in as you wanted, and put the fear of God into her. Once she knew we had reason to suspect her, she might well have stopped.'

Tansey hesitated. Daphne Mariner had told him about the last threatening telephone call that Mrs Randelson had made and how she had responded, calling the woman by name. Personally, he believed this might well have prompted Mrs

Randelson's final suicidal attack on the Rocques, but he decided it was more diplomatic not to mention all this to Midvale.

Instead, he said, 'I doubt if it would have made any difference, sir. She was obsessed with her desire for revenge. I wouldn't be in the least surprised if she hadn't been lying in wait for some days for the Rocques' car to go past. It was chance she got all three of them, but killed the wrong one. There's very little one can do in that sort of case.'

'I expect you're right.' Midvale sighed. 'I'm sorry about Bertram. He was a good man, though not very practical. Incidentally, I gather the Manor is to be sold at a knock-down price, and that by the time all the debts are paid, Lady Rocque won't get a penny. Still, I suppose you might call that a kind of justice.'

But justice wasn't yet done with Andrea Rocque.

Six months later, Chief Inspector Tansey received a brief note from Simon Wayne. Attached was a newspaper clipping from a northern newspaper. It said that the actress Andrea Marston had been sentenced to five years' imprisonment for injuring a police officer when driving a car while under the influence of drink, and failing to stop at the scene of the accident. Her alcohol test had been three times that permitted.

Simon had written: *Christopher and Daphne are on their honeymoon, and I shan't bother to send them this, but I thought you would like to know. It's usually only in fiction that a case is rounded off so neatly, isn't it?*